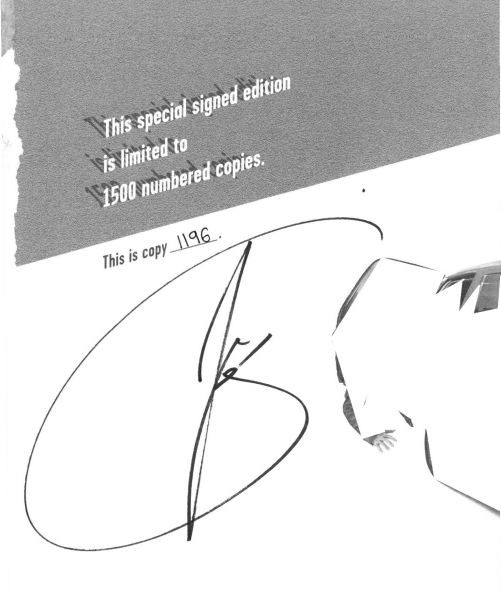

This special signed edition
is limited to
1500 numbered copies.

This is copy 1196.

JOHN SCALZI

The
DISPATCHER:
Travel by Bullet

The DISPATCHER:
Travel by Bullet

JOHN
SCALZI

SUBTERRANEAN PRESS 2023

First Print Edition

ISBN
978-1-64524-081-5

Subterranean Press
PO Box 190106
Burton, MI 48519

subterraneanpress.com

Manufactured in the United States of America

CHAPTER ONE

It was 2:48 p.m. on a Tuesday, and I was about to do the same thing for the third time since I began work at noon: convince some distraught people that I shouldn't, in fact, kill their loved one.

"Mr. Szymanski, Mrs. Szymanski," I said to the couple clinging to each other in the waiting room of Northwestern Memorial's Critical Care Unit. I kept my distance and didn't shake hands. "I'm Tony Valdez. I'm the on-duty dispatcher for the CCU here." I held up a folder. "I understand you've requested a dispatch for Joseph Szymanski, who's your father, yes, Mr. Szymanski?"

"That's right," Mrs. Szymanski said, before her husband could reply. She was not interrupting her husband; Mr. Szymanski had a shell-shocked look that suggested he was not going to be answering much of anything. I could sympathize, but I was also on the clock, and I had at least one more family to see for the same discussion. I turned my attention to Mrs. Szymanski.

"May I sit?" I pointed to a chair across from the couple. Northwestern Memorial had actively discouraged visiting the Critical Care Unit except in cases where medical decisions had to be made, and even then they encouraged family members to phone in. This was the residue of the recent pandemic, which we had only just gotten to the other side of. The Szymanskis had decided to show up anyway. Some people just had to be there. Again, I could sympathize.

"Mrs. Szymanski," I began.

"Joanna," she said.

"Joanna," I continued, "before we do or say anything else, I want to make sure we're on the same page here in terms of what you're asking for, and what I'm able to do for your father-in-law. Is that all right?"

"Yes."

"Okay," I said. "Now, you understand what a dispatcher does, yes?"

"If someone's about to die, you fix it so they come back and they can get better," Joanna Szymanski said.

I nodded. "That's essentially correct." It was, in truth, only vaguely correct. The way I "fixed" someone who was about to die of natural or accidental causes was to kill them myself. Their death then became intentional, the work of a human agent. For more than a dozen years now, when someone went out of their way to kill someone else, nine hundred and ninety-nine times out of a thousand, they came back. How and why this was happening was fodder for scientists and philosophers and religious figures. The practical and medical aspects of it were why I had a job.

"So you can fix Joe and bring him back," Joanna Szymanski pressed.

"It's essentially correct," I repeated. "But it's also a little more complicated than that." I held up the file I had for Joseph Szymanski, which the hospital was required to give me for evaluation. "It's the complications here that I want to go over with you."

"The law says you *have* to help us." She looked at me with a set jaw, visible even through her mask, and I imagined Joanna Szymanski did not lose a whole lot of arguments with anyone. This was fine. I was not here to argue with her.

"Yes," I agreed. "At the beginning of the recent pandemic, the State of Illinois passed the Family Compassion Act, which among other things gives families the right to request dispatch for affected next of kin when there is no superseding Do Not Resuscitate request on file. This request can overrule the direction of the affected's doctor or insurer." I recited this like I had said it a few dozen times in the recent past, because I *had* done just that. There was a reasonably good chance I could recite it in my sleep at this point. "If you and your husband formally request this dispatch, I must and will perform it, Joanna. Don't worry about that."

She relaxed slightly; she had been expecting a fight.

"But I need to explain to you why a dispatch might not be the right option here."

That tensed her right up again.

I continued before she could object. "Again, if you request the dispatch, I'll provide it. But I want you to understand what I do and how what I do works. First, let's be very clear that what you're asking me to do is to kill your father-in-law."

"He'll come back, though," she said.

"Usually, yes. But there's a small chance he might not. About one in a thousand. It's a small risk, but it's a real risk. In the time since Illinois passed the Family Compassion Act, ten people who were dispatched died because of it. You have to accept there's a chance your father-in-law might be the eleventh."

"If he is, he'll be better than he is right now." She looked at her husband. "Bill has a coworker whose dad was dispatched last year, and when he came back, they shot him up with all sorts of medicine and got his viral load way down."

"That can happen," I agreed. "I don't know the details of that case so I can't speak to it." I raised the file in my hand again. "I've looked at your father-in-law's case. It says he had an accident at home, and that he's been on a respirator here for a week."

"Yes. So?"

"In a successful dispatch, when people return, their bodies typically reset to an earlier time," I said. "It's why I can do what I do. If someone's having surgery and it's not working out, I dispatch them and they come back to a state just before the surgery, and the doctors can try again. But it's important to know the 'reset' here is usually only the equivalent of a few hours. A day at most. If I successfully dispatch your father-in-law, he'll go back to the state he was in this morning. Or yesterday at the earliest."

"That's still better than he is *now*, for Christ's sake," Joanna said.

"It might be," I said. "But you have to understand that when I dispatch someone, they don't stay here, at the hospital. They return to the place they feel the safest in, and most attached to. That's usually their home, but it might be elsewhere. Did your father-in-law live alone?"

"He's been in the same house for forty years."

"Then that's where he'll likely go. When he arrives, he'll be naked—clothes and personal effects don't follow—and he'll be alone, unless family is there waiting for him. Now, Joanna, your father-in-law is on a respirator for a reason. It's the same reason he was on it this morning, and yesterday. When I dispatch him, if he comes back, he won't have the respirator helping him breathe anymore."

"You're saying bringing him back might kill him anyway."

"I'm saying I want to make sure you understand what you're asking for," I repeated. "If everything works, your father-in-law will go home, but in my professional opinion the chances are he'll be right back here within a couple of hours. If the EMTs can get to him. If he can get back here to the CCU at all."

"The law says the hospital has to readmit him," she said.

"Northwestern Memorial will readmit him, yes," I said. "But there will still be a gap in the care. They'll take care of him, and there's no better hospital in Chicago than this one. But think about what I'm saying to you, that this *is* the best hospital in Chicago, and there's a very good chance his outcome will be worse than if he stayed here."

"You think we should just keep him on the respirator until he dies."

"I think you and your husband should make your decision based on the best available information. By law, I can and will dispatch your father-in-law. At least now you have my professional opinion on the risks and likely outcomes. I'll do what you want me to do. You have to ask yourselves now what will be best for your father-in-law. For Joe."

For the first time since I sat down, I saw in Joanna Szymanski's eyes a glimmer of doubt. She had heard what I said and was beginning to weigh the options.

"Do it," Bill Szymanski said.

"Bill." Joanna put a hand on his arm.

"No," he said to his wife. "He's been here for two weeks. On that damn machine for a week. We haven't been able to see him or talk to him. He's alone. He hates hospitals. He should be at home."

"He might die," Joanna said.

"Then he'll die at home," Bill said, eyes welling up. "He'll die with family around him. He'll die looking at the picture of Mom he has on his nightstand. It won't be here, with a tube down his throat." He looked over at me. "Do it. Dispatch him."

I looked over to Joanna. "You're both listed to make medical decisions. Both of you have to agree."

She nodded silently, still holding on to her husband's arm.

I stood up. "Do you have anyone who can be at his house?"

"Bill's sister is already there. She's watching the dog. Bill's other sister is just down the block."

"Let them know he's on the way," I said. "I'll be making the dispatch in the next fifteen minutes."

Bill Szymanski started sobbing openly. I turned to go.

"Mr. Valdez," Joanna said.

I turned.

"Thank you."

I smiled tightly and walked into the CCU.

"How'd it go?" Anita Cain asked. She was the nurse who was assisting me on the shift. She'd been waiting for me while I spoke to the Szymanskis.

"They want a dispatch," I said.

"You explained it to them, right? The whole 'you're just going to make it worse' thing?"

"I always do," I said. "It doesn't help."

"There oughta be a law."

"There is one," I pointed out. "That's the problem." There wasn't a dispatcher who didn't hate the Family Compassion Act, or the variations of it that had popped up in other states during the pandemic but then stayed on the books after the crisis passed. The argument for these laws in the state legislatures was that it gave more control and comfort to families during a traumatic time, which at first meant the pandemic and then afterward meant pretty much whatever anyone wanted it to.

The argument against it, which the representatives of the dispatchers duly gave, was that it was medical theater that only offered the illusion of control, and it obliged dispatchers to perform dispatches they knew to be unsafe and unethical. These arguments had the effect of making dispatchers look heartless to people who had never had to deal with the aftereffects of an ill-advised dispatch.

"He's over here," Cain said, leading me to a semi-private room.

Joseph Szymanski's room had two other patients in it, each with their own ventilator—each of them, like Szymanski, sedated to keep them from clawing the tubes out of their throats in a panic.

Cain drew the curtains around Szymanski's bed and then pointed to a side table. "Your equipment," she said.

"You already placed it?" I asked.

"I figured you would go three for three."

The two other families I had spoken to on this shift had also elected for dispatching.

"It's not a good record," I said, as I unwrapped the applicator from its sterile packaging. "The applicator" was a very bland way to describe the device I would place up against Szymanski's soft palate to launch an exploding pellet into his brain. The dispatching profession liked its euphemisms. It was why I was called a dispatcher and not "a killer hired by insurance companies and hospitals."

"Ready," I said to Cain. She began to remove the tubes from Szymanski's throat. As she did, I gave him a quick once-over. He was in his seventies, but still solid in that Chicago Polish way. He was the sort of guy who looked like he never once left the city limits, because why would he, when they've got the Bears and the White Sox, and everyone he ever knew or would know all lived in his southwest Chicago neighborhood.

"They were right about one thing," I said.

"What's that?" Cain asked.

"He'd probably want to die at home."

"Is he going to?"

"We'll find out."

Cain nodded at this and finished up her work. "Clear," she said.

I put the applicator in Joseph Szymanski's mouth and settled it into place.

"Good luck, Joe," I said, and delivered the payload.

There was a pause, and then Joseph Szymanski disappeared, leaving behind his hospital gown and a soft *pop* as air rushed in to fill the space where his body used to be. That meant that somewhere in Chicago, probably in his bed, Szymanski would reappear, naked and unventilated.

I decided not to think of him and what he would be feeling after that.

"What's next?" Cain asked.

"Another family to discuss a dispatch request with," I said. "The Gianellis. At four. This one on a Zoom call."

"Does being on a Zoom call make it any easier?"

"Not really," I said.

"It's a heck of a job you've got here, Tony."

"Well," I said, "the real irony is that I was supposed to have another job by now."

"You were going to quit dispatching? And leave all this behind?"

"Not exactly," I said. "I was supposed to be Chicago PD's first full-time dispatcher. Help them solve dispatch-related crimes. On the actual payroll."

"But then the pandemic happened?"

"Then the pandemic happened," I agreed. "And it was all hands on deck at the hospitals. And the police decided they had other things to spend their money on in a crisis."

"At least we have jobs," Cain said, drawing back the curtains from Szymanski's now-empty bed. "My sister was laid off at the start of the pandemic, and her job never came back when it was over. I'm paying for her groceries and rent. I'm not loving that."

"It's good she has you," I said.

"Sure. All I have to do is not get sick myself."

I was going to respond, but then a man in scrubs appeared at the door of the room.

"Tony Valdez?" he said, looking at me.

"That's me."

"You're needed in the ER right now."

I furrowed my brow. "I thought Ella Cross was working the ER." Ella was a newer dispatcher. I hadn't spent any real time with her, but she seemed more than competent.

"She is," the man in scrubs said.

"So what's the problem?"

"The problem is, the guy we just rolled in to the ER asked for you. He's a real mess and he won't let us work on him until he talks to you. If you don't hurry, he'll be dead. Maybe hurry."

CHAPTER
TWO

The man who asked for me in the emergency room looked like he'd been rubbed across half a mile of the Dan Ryan Expressway—in part, I was told, because he had. That he wasn't already dead was some small miracle. That he was still conscious was a different sort of miracle, and not one of the good ones.

The physician attending him, who looked more harried than the usual ER attending, saw me looking at him. Her tag identified her as Rebecca Harper. "Do you know this man?" she asked, coming up to me.

I looked more closely.

It was Mason Schilling.

"I know him," I said.

"Is he family?"

"Not exactly," I said. Mason Schilling was a dispatcher like me. Unlike me, he preferred to do his work in the legal margins of the profession. That was a place I some-times found myself out of necessity, but avoided when less ethically nebulous work options were available. Mason and I had a personal and professional history. The personal history was okay. The professional history was problematic. "He's a friend," I concluded.

"Well, okay, your friend here has six broken ribs on one side of his body, two broken ribs on the other, a punctured lung, one broken arm, two broken legs, and more internal bleeding than is probably survivable. Plus a whole lot of his skin was left on the pavement."

I motioned with my head to the guy who had come to get me. "He said Mason fell out of a car on the Dan Ryan."

"'Fell' in the sense of opening a door and rolling out, sure," Dr. Harper said. "The EMTs said that's what eye-witnesses told them."

"That would explain his injuries."

"That and then immediately getting hit by a Tesla, yes." Harper glanced at Mason. "When you talk to your friend, you might tell him there are easier and less pain-ful ways of ending it all."

This got my attention. "He told you he was commit-ting suicide?"

Harper shook her head. "He hasn't told us anything. When he was rolled in, he asked what hospital he was at. When we told him, he asked for you and wouldn't let us work on him or let Ella do her thing." She pointed over to Ella Cross, the ER dispatcher, who was standing several feet away, looking vaguely irritated—either at Mason, or at my presence, or both. "At this point we're waiting for him to pass out so we can work on him anyway, but he just won't lose consciousness."

In spite of everything I smiled grimly. "That's very much in Mason's personality."

"Well, you're here now. So talk to him, and please tell him to either let us fix him, or let you dispatch him. We have other patients to get to."

By this time I could see Mason looking at me. He knew I was there.

I nodded to Harper. "Tell everyone to give us a little privacy for a couple of minutes."

"If he codes we're coming in."

"That's fine," I said.

She clapped her hands and then asked everyone crowding around Mason to back off. They did.

I got in close to Mason. His face was mostly abrasions. "I'm here," I said.

The response was barely whispered, as befitted a man with a punctured lung. "About time," he said.

"I heard you threw yourself out of a moving car."

"Yeah."

"You want to tell me why?" I asked.

"It was the best choice at the moment," he said.

"That's not a great choice."

"It might have worked, except for that Tesla."

"Mason," I said. "You're dying. Let these people help you."

Mason twitched, the barest amount, which I understood to be a shake of his head. "No point," he said.

I nodded toward Ella Cross, who was still lingering, out of earshot. "Then let her dispatch you."

"Can't."

I frowned at this. "What do you mean you can't?"

Mason grabbed me suddenly, with what I hoped was his unbroken arm, and drew me even closer to him. "There's nowhere safe," he said.

I pulled back, looking at him, thinking about what he had just said.

It's popularly assumed that when someone gets dispatched, they return to their home, and for nearly every person that's true. But in actuality, what happens is that someone who is dispatched returns to the place they feel the safest, wherever that may be. Sometimes that's not home. But it's somewhere the dispatched person knows, and knows to be safe for them.

Mason was telling me that nowhere he could think of returning to was safe for him. Nowhere.

I recognized that this belief of Mason's was not what you would call existential in nature. What he was saying was that no matter where he might return, someone or something was waiting for him.

I leaned back in. "What have you gotten yourself into this time?"

After a second a noise came out of him that I didn't quite place. Then it happened again, and I realized that he was trying to laugh.

"So you would rather die than go back to whoever's waiting for you," I said.

"Yes," Mason whispered.

"You don't need me here to tell them that you want to die."

"I need you to make sure it happens," Mason said.

I nodded. Dr. Harper was waiting to try to save him as soon as he lost consciousness; Ella Cross would not hesitate to dispatch him if Harper told her she was out of options. Mason almost certainly didn't have a Do Not Resuscitate order on file with the hospital or with an insurer—that wouldn't have been his style—so the medical team could make efforts on his behalf unless someone was making sure they didn't. His verbal orders might be seen as coming from someone not in his right mind, unless I was there to attest that he was. Or had been.

Which I was willing to do. But something still troubled me. "Were you trying to commit suicide when you jumped out of that car?" I asked Mason.

"No," he whispered. "Thought I could get away."

"By rolling out of a car on the Dan Ryan."

"What I had to work with."

I looked at Mason. "You could've done legit gigs, you know."

Another attempt at a laugh. "Boring," he said.

I was at a loss. Mason and I were not what you would call close anymore. Our choices of work focus had taken us further apart, and I fell in with the cops, who Mason was mostly happy to avoid. But the fact was, Mason never turned me away when I needed something from him. He would criticize, or at least comment sardonically, on my work choices and how I would choose to present myself. When it came down to it, however, he would help.

I wanted to help him now. He was choosing death over whatever else was waiting for him, not because he wanted to die, but because, like rolling out of a moving vehicle on the freeway, it was the best option available to him.

"What else can I do for you?" I asked.

"Hold my hand," Mason said.

I reached over and took the hand of his unbroken arm.

"The other one," he whispered.

I walked over to the other side of the bed and took his other hand. Mason grimaced as I clutched it and then relaxed.

"Here it comes," Mason said a minute later, in a strange and wavering whisper.

It, I knew, was death. I had been in hospitals and among the critically ill and injured enough in my career to be aware that often the dying could feel it coming for them. Mason was letting me know it was headed his way, and wouldn't be long now.

It was then that a thought came to me.

I bent down and whispered that thought into what was left of Mason's ear.

Ten seconds later, Mason lightly squeezed my hand. Good enough.

"Ms. Cross," I said.

She came over instantly. "Yes?"

"Mason's consented to a dispatching," I said.

She cocked her head. "And you want to perform it?"

"No," I said. "You're the ER dispatcher." Cross's face lightened a little at this; she appreciated me acknowledging her role. "But if you don't mind, I'll hold his hand while you do it. It's what he asked me to do."

Cross nodded and called for assistance. Two seconds later Harper was holding open Mason's mouth while Cross unwrapped the applicator and pressed it into my friend's mouth. She did a five count.

At "two" I felt Mason squeeze my hand again.

Then Cross used the applicator to deliver the payload.

The next five seconds felt like an hour.

And then Mason disappeared.

I clenched my hand, which was now suddenly clean of all the blood Mason had smeared into it. It had gone to wherever it was that Mason had gone, hopefully back into Mason, and in usable form. I put my hand in my pocket and then turned to Cross.

"Thank you," I said. She bowed her head slightly to acknowledge my thanks.

"How'd you get him to agree to be dispatched?" Harper wanted to know.

"I didn't," I said. "I just allowed him to do what he wanted to do."

"Which was?"

"Not die."

Harper smiled ruefully at this. "That should've taken less time."

"The important thing is it happened."

"I *suppose*," she said.

I decided not to follow this up. "Unless there's anything else, Doctor, I'll get back to my actual duties."

"Actually, there is something else," Harper said. "While you were talking to your friend, a cop showed up. A detective. She wants to talk to you. She says she knows you."

I looked up and past Harper to the doorway of the ER, to see the cop in question.

Detective Nona Langdon.

"Yes, I know her," I said.

"You seem to know a lot of people, Mr. Valdez," Harper said.

"You have no idea, Dr. Harper," I replied.

THREE

"This feels familiar," I said to Nona Langdon, as I walked up to her.

"I get that," she said. She and I had met a few years back in this same hospital, when she had come to me about a case involving another dispatcher. Time is cyclical.

I motioned toward the outdoors. "Come on. Let's get out of their way."

We walked out of the ER and into the outside world, toward Erie Street. I found one of the building pillars and drew in a deep breath.

Langdon noticed. "Long day?"

"Long day," I agreed. "Long week. Long month. Long *year*. I spend my time trying to convince family members not to have me dispatch their parent, or sibling, or uncle, or whoever, and they don't listen because they feel like they should be doing *something*, and a dispatch feels like something. And I want to yell at them that 'something' isn't the same as 'something useful,' but it wouldn't do any good."

"This have to do with that Family Compassion Act thing?"

"Yup."

"It was a very popular bill, if I remember correctly."

"Sure," I said. "And even some dispatchers thought it was okay at first. Suddenly we all had more work than we could handle."

"And now?"

"I feel like a doctor trying to explain why you don't give antibiotics for the flu." I glanced at my watch. "And I'm going to have to do it again in the near future, so you should probably get to whatever you were going to ask me about now."

"All right," Langdon said. "Your friend Mason Schilling."

"Yes."

"Who you just dispatched."

"I did not, actually," I said. "Ella Cross did. Her department. Her call."

"So what were you doing there?"

"He asked to see me."

"And why did he do that?"

I shrugged. "Existential crisis?"

"Is that a question to me?" she said.

"No, sorry, I meant he was close to death and was frightened."

"Even though he's a dispatcher."

"Being a dispatcher doesn't make you immune to the fear of death, I assure you," I said. "If anything, it brings it that much closer to home."

Langdon had a small smile for this. "So he wanted one of his own kind around."

"He wanted a friend, yes. That I'm a dispatcher is incidental."

"Will Ella Cross tell me the same thing?"

"She'll tell you he didn't consent to being dispatched until he spoke to me," I said. "Otherwise, yes."

"That's interesting," Langdon said. "You had to convince him to be dispatched."

"Like I said, an existential crisis."

"An existential crisis entirely unrelated to him throwing himself out of a car while it was on the Dan Ryan, right?"

"Oh, you heard," I said.

"Not only have I heard, I've seen the video," Langdon said. "From several different dash cams, including the one on the Tesla that smacked into him immediately afterward."

"How was it?"

"Not pleasant. The good news, if you want to call it that, is the Dan Ryan never moves that quickly during daylight, and the Tesla has that anti-collision software. The car your friend threw himself out of wasn't going fast enough that his exit would kill him, and the Tesla was slowing down when it hit him. Today's his lucky day."

I smirked at this. "I wouldn't call a dozen broken bones and a punctured lung 'lucky.'"

"Then he's lucky you convinced him to be dispatched. That should solve all of those problems. For now, anyway."

"What does that mean?" I asked.

"When you were talking to Schilling, did he happen to explain to you why he launched himself out of a moving car?"

"He had a punctured lung," I said. "He wasn't talking in detail about anything."

"That's not a 'no,' Tony," Langdon noted.

"Sorry. I'm not trying to be coy. No, he didn't tell me what made him throw himself out of a car. He said something about it being the best option available at the time, but didn't explain why."

"And you don't have any idea what he was doing with himself just prior to that? What gigs he might have taken?"

"Mason understood a while back that it would probably be best if he didn't give me all the details of his professional life," I said. "In no small part because I worked with you, and was actually planning to join the police force in the near future."

"He didn't want to incriminate himself."

"Yes, that," I agreed. "But also, he didn't want to make things difficult for me. He didn't approve of me joining the cops. He thought it was a waste of opportunity. But he wasn't going to make himself an obstacle to that, either. Not that it mattered, as it turned out." I waved in the direction of the Emergency Room.

"The pandemic changed the direction of a lot of lives," Langdon observed.

"That it did," I said, nodding. "Dispatchers included."

"But not Mason Schilling's," Langdon said. "All the rest of you dispatchers were assigned to hospitals to help with the crisis. But he's not on the schedule of any hospital in the Chicagoland area. He turned away guaranteed work."

"I don't know about that," I said.

"I do."

I reassessed Langdon. "This isn't just about Mason falling out of a car, is it?"

"I never said it was."

I sighed. "I really don't know what he was up to," I said. "The rest of us went back to work in the hospitals when the pandemic hit because there were legit jobs open again, and because we were told that Illinois might pull our licenses to dispatch if we didn't. Carrot and stick, you might say. But it wouldn't surprise me if Mason decided he could dodge the stick and keep on the shadier side of things."

"Why is that?"

"Because he'd then have the shady side to himself, for one thing. At least for a while. Anyway, you can ask him. He's been dispatched. He's probably at home."

"That's where I'm going next," Langdon said. "I just wanted to see if you had anything for me at all."

"Nothing as a dispatcher," I said. "And as his friend, all I did was hold his hand while he was dispatched."

Langdon blinked at this. "You held his hand."

"Existential crisis," I reminded her.

"I guess."

"Do you have anything on the car he flung himself out of?" I asked.

"A black Cadillac Escalade, later model, Illinois plates," Langdon said. "It got off the expressway after Schilling exited. We got the plates off various dash cams. They're registered to a Toyota Camry that was wrecked a couple of years ago. The owner of that car works at a Starbucks at O'Hare. She's clean. We're following up."

"Okay."

"There's another thing," Langdon said.

"Of course there is," I said. I wanted that to come out jokingly but didn't manage it.

"Do you know who Paul Cooper is?"

"The name doesn't ring a bell, no."

"He's a tech billionaire. Created a cryptocurrency trading app called MoreCoinz."

"I've seen it advertised," I said. "I don't use it."

"Just as well," Langdon said. "He's dead. Suicide, apparently."

"Apparently? How is there doubt?"

"There was a party. It was at the apartment of Gabrielle Friedkin, in that development her family has going up in Old Town."

"I've seen ads for it, too," I said. Gentrification was never-ending, although the pandemic had slowed it down.

"Lots of people saw Cooper at the party. People remembered him, aside from the fact that he's a billionaire, because like a good nerd, he had brought his laptop with him to a party."

"That would be memorable," I agreed. "Sad, but memorable."

"Yes, well. It's not the only thing he brought. He showed up with a revolver as well. And as the party was winding down, he shot himself. Or at least that's what it looked like to the witnesses."

"All right," I said. "And?"

"And it's a high-profile incident featuring several of Chicago's richest citizens, so the on-scene investigation was a little more thorough than it might otherwise have been. And when we talked to some of the party guests, one of them mentioned seeing your friend Mason Schilling there. We went to talk to him, but he wasn't around. Turns out he was ejecting himself from an SUV with fake plates on the expressway at the time."

"That's an interesting set of coincidences," I said neutrally.

Langdon smiled. "I'm not at all surprised to hear you say that. Anyway. We'll be looking for him. On the off chance you see him before we do, you might suggest to him that he should speak to us at his earliest possible convenience."

"I don't think he's likely to take your advice on that," I said. "At least not without a lawyer present."

"Possibly not. But your friend is throwing himself out of moving vehicles. Perhaps it's time he should re-evaluate his life choices."

I grinned at this. "I'll let him know you said that if I see him."

"Do that," Langdon said. "And take care of yourself, Tony. You're looking worn down."

"Thanks," I said. "I'm feeling worn down."

"When all this is over, maybe you can still come work for us. Rumor is, our funding might start going up again."

"When all of this is over, I'm going to sleep for a year," I said. "We'll see what I do after that."

Langdon left me there, leaning on that pillar.

After a few more minutes of just breathing, I went back inside and had that Zoom call with the Gianellis. As small miracles would have it, they actually listened to what I had to say about their mother, Angela, currently on a respirator in a room not far from where Joe Szymanski had been. They decided to think about it and call the hospital the next day with their decision. Well, I wasn't going to be working then, so one of the other dispatchers would get the call, if they decided to go through with it. Given the day I'd had so far, I was all right with that.

My shift ended at eight. I splurged and took a Lyft home to Wicker Park. On the way I ordered from the local Lou Malnati's for a thin crust sausage and parmesan wings. I walked home from the carryout, allowing the cheese on the pizza just enough time not to blister the roof of my mouth when I bit into it.

I had stayed in Wicker Park after my former apartment had burned down in a fire. It wasn't the neighborhood's fault, after all. My current apartment was a condo off of North Avenue, in a building that I couldn't have afforded—except that the actual condo owner was subletting it to me on very reasonable terms while he did an extended overseas employment jaunt. There's something to be said for having successful college friends. He couldn't come home in the pandemic, anyway.

I juggled food while I maneuvered my keys into the lock, first for the building door and then to my door on the second floor. Once inside, I deposited the food on the table and then locked and latched the door.

"I hope you like Lou Malnati's," I said.

"It's all right," Mason Schilling said. He was on my couch, in my bathrobe. He noticed me eyeing the robe. "I didn't think you would mind," he said. "The alternative was rubbing my bare ass all over your apartment."

"It's fine," I said.

"I didn't know if it would work," Mason said. "You telling me that your apartment was safe, I mean."

"I didn't know if it would work either," I said.

Mason shrugged. "The other option was 'or death.' Figured it was worth a chance."

"I'm glad you did."

"Well, so am I, if I'm being honest." Mason frowned. "For as long as it lasts, anyway. Someone will eventually figure this out."

"Eventually," I agreed. I reached into my pants pocket and fished out the object Mason had given me as I held his hand when he was dispatched. "In the meantime, you can tell me what this is. And why my apartment is the only safe place in the world for you right now."

FOUR

Mason held his hand out for the object. "Can I have it back?"

I shook my head. "I think I want answers to some questions first."

"That's entirely reasonable," Mason replied. "And it might actually be smarter for me *not* to have that on me for a while. And you might not want to let people know it exists."

"Why is that?"

"This is going to take some explaining." Mason pointed at the pizza box. "Can we eat while we talk? Coming back from the dead makes me hungry."

"There was food in the apartment."

"I didn't know if you wanted me going through your fridge."

"Mason, I told you my place was safe for you. I think that would extend to you having a *snack*."

"You never know. Some people are touchy." He opened the pizza box, got out a slice, and sat back down on the couch. "That object in your hand," he said between bites, "is payment. And tips."

I frowned at this. "Tips."

"Yeah."

"As in some information? Or as in a gratuity?"

"Gratuity."

I looked at this object again. It was a small block of plastic with a connector attached to it. It looked like your basic USB thumb drive. "There's money in this?"

"It's a crypto wallet. It's got a certain amount of cryptocurrency on it." He pointed to the drive. "In this case, something called 'MajicBienz,' and that's spelled like whoever named it failed the third grade."

I nodded at this. "It's not a legit cryptocurrency if it's not badly spelled."

"Drives me nuts," Mason said. "It's like people naming their kid 'Ashley' or 'Braden,' but then spelling the name with six y's. It doesn't make the kid special. It just means they won't be able to spell their own name until they're in high school."

"So, what's the real world value of your magic beans?" I asked, wagging the key between my fingers.

"Well, that's the question, isn't it?" Mason said. "Yesterday morning, a whole MajicBien was selling for forty-two hundred dollars. But MajicBienz are a really volatile currency, so right this instant it could be worth a tenth of that, or three times that. That's the 'fun' of crypto, Tony. You never know how much you're worth at any moment. I'll find out when I plug it in to my computer and transfer it into my account on MoreCoinz." He took another bite of his pizza.

"That doesn't sound like you, Mason," I said. "You're usually one for cash on the barrelhead, no credit, no funny stuff. And nothing traceable, ever."

"The people I was doing my thing for don't carry cash, Tony. It's doubtful any of them have actually touched paper money in a decade." He pointed at the pizza box. "Shit, they even pay for *takeout* through crypto transfers. It's kind of their *thing*."

"So what convinced you to go along?"

"Because when you add up the tips as well as the fee, I got about forty thousand dollars for one night's work. Well. Forty thousand at the time. It may be more or less now."

"That's not bad," I allowed.

"It's not the first time I've made that much, either."

"This explains why you weren't in a rush to take a dispatching job with a hospital."

"You folks seem to be getting along without me," Mason said, around his pizza slice.

"Not really," I said. "It's a mess."

"All the more reason for me to stay out of it. You know I don't exactly have a cheerful bedside manner."

"Maybe. On the other hand, none of the rest of us have felt the need to jump out of a moving car."

Mason chuckled at this. "Fair point," he said. He turned his attention back to his pizza.

"You going to explain that?" I asked.

"The jumping out of a moving car?"

I nodded.

"I already told you about that. It was the best option in the moment."

"Yes, you did say that. What you're leaving out is *why* it was the best option."

"Maybe it's best for you if you're not involved, Tony."

I motioned around my apartment. "You're here. I'm kind of involved."

"There's involved and then there's *involved*," Mason said. "Right now, you're the first. You can still avoid the second. I can be out of your hair this evening if you want."

"Mason," I said, "you don't even have pants right now."

"I figure you might let me borrow a pair."

"We're not the same size."

"I can suck it in for a few hours."

"And then there's the reason you're here in the first place, which is there's literally nowhere else safe for you right now," I reminded him. "You need help, Mason.

I'm happy to help you. But you have to *let* me help you. Which means telling me what's going on with you."

Mason opened his mouth, and then closed it again. "Damn it," he said.

I got it. "You don't want me in your business," I said.

"I really don't," he admitted. "No offense, Tony."

"None taken."

"It's not just you. I don't want anyone in my business right now."

"Because it's not safe."

"That's not why. I just don't like people in my business in the best of times. But yeah. It's not safe, also."

"Let me make it easier for you," I said. "I heard about Paul Cooper."

Mason stopped mid-chew to stare at me. "Well, fuck," he said, after a minute.

"Well, fuck, indeed," I agreed. "So, are you finally going to give me some details? Or do I have to take away your pizza?"

Mason opened his mouth to answer just as the door buzzer went off. He looked at me, and for the first time I'd known him, I saw fear in his eyes.

"You expecting someone?" he asked.

"No," I said. I went over to the intercom connected to the door buzzer. "Hello?"

"Anthony Valdez?" A man's voice came from the speaker.

"Who's asking for him?"

"I'm Andy Liu, and I'm with the Chicago office of the Federal Bureau of Investigation. I'm investigating the disappearance of your friend Mason Schilling. I understand you were one of the last people to see him alive. I was hoping we might be able to have a chat."

"Again, I apologize for bothering you this late in evening," Agent Liu said to me a few moments later, well away from my apartment. "I tried to get in touch with you at the hospital but you'd already left."

"It's not a problem," I said. "You gave me an excuse to get out of the apartment and get ice cream."

The two of us were standing in front of Zooabaloo, an ice cream shop on North Avenue. Its conceit was that all the ice cream was related to, and mostly shaped like, animals. It was very Wicker Park. I took Agent Liu there because I very much did not want him to see who was in my home, and also, despite the silly conceit of the shop, Zooabaloo had really excellent desserts.

"And how is it?" Agent Liu pointed to my cup of ice cream, which was meant to have the face of a tiger, and did, sort of, until I attacked it with the biodegradable bamboo spoon Zooabaloo provided.

"It's good," I said. I showed it to him. "It's called Tiger Tail ice cream. Orange and black licorice. It's big in Canada."

"Canada is weird," Liu said.

"It's an acquired taste," I allowed. I tilted the cup toward him; the ruined face of the tiger considered him with a single baleful candy eye. "Want to try it?"

Liu held up a hand. "Lactose intolerant. And I don't like black licorice."

"Reasonable on the first, cowardly on the second."

Liu smiled. "Guilty."

"So why does the FBI have an interest in Mason, anyway?" I asked, shifting gears now that we had established a comfortable rapport. I have watched Nona Langdon enough when she was doing her police interviews, so the skill had begun to rub off. Also, I figured the longer I kept Liu from actually being in charge of the questions, the better off I would be.

"He's a material witness in an investigation."

"That sounds serious."

"There's a reason I'm bothering you at almost nine p.m."

"What's the investigation?"

"Among other things, a possible murder."

I stopped mid-swallow of my tiger tail ice cream. "Come again?"

"Murder."

"Murder's a state charge."

"It usually is," Liu said. "Sometimes it's not."

"Also, murder is not exactly common anymore. I'm a dispatcher. I know this."

"It's not common. But it still happens. As a dispatcher, you should know *that.*"

"Are you accusing Mason of murder?" I asked.

"Is there a reason you think I would be?" Liu replied.

Shit, walked into that, I thought. The question ball in the conversation was now in Liu's possession.

"All I know is that he showed up in our ER this afternoon."

"Yes. After jumping out of a car at high speed."

"He did it on the Dan Ryan. It wasn't *that* high speed."

"High speed enough to need a dispatch," Liu pointed out. "That's not the act of a man who's in a good place with his life, Mr. Valdez."

"Are you an FBI agent or a therapist, Agent Liu?"

"Actually I do have a degree in psychology," Liu said. "It occasionally comes in handy in this job. One of the reasons the FBI recruited me."

"Mason never struck me as the murdering type," I said.

"Nor I, from what I know of him. I've read his file."

"Mason has an FBI file?"

"Every dispatcher has an FBI file, Mr. Valdez," Liu said. "You're all professional killers. We're obliged to keep track of that."

"I don't know how to feel about this," I said.

"It's not that big of a deal. I've read your file, too. You'll be glad to know the Bureau thinks you're mostly harmless."

"Uh...thanks."

"You should stay away from Brennan Tunney more than you do, though."

"I'll keep that in mind," I said. Brennan Tunney, ostensibly a businessman, came from a long line of Irish mob bosses. He maintained that these days his businesses were entirely legitimate, a claim that might even be true. But just because those businesses were legitimate didn't mean everything he did to keep them running was entirely legal. Our paths had crossed a few times in previous years, which resulted in him having me killed at one point, and owing me a favor at another. He still owed me that favor, come to think of it. I had no intention of collecting.

"Mason Schilling's FBI file, on the other hand, is *sizable*," Liu noted.

"I don't know anything about that."

"I suspect *that's* not entirely true, but I think it's accurate that you don't know everything he's been up to. So let me fill you in just a little, Mr. Valdez. Have you heard of Paul Cooper?"

"He's a billionaire," I said. "Made some money off a cryptocurrency app."

"He's also dead," Liu said.

"I'd heard that, too."

"The thing is, Cooper wasn't just some billionaire. His app handles a significant percentage of all crypto trading that goes on in the U.S. All the trading that's done openly, anyway. Mostly from people with more money than sense, or who think they're going to get rich investing in something they can't spell and don't actually understand how it works."

"You could say the same about the stock market," I pointed out.

"The stock market has the SEC watching over it," Liu said. "Crypto mostly doesn't. There's a lot that's shady going on in that sector. A lot of people are going to lose their shirts, and their homes, and so on."

I nodded. "So you were investigating Cooper."

"No. Confidentially, Cooper was working for us."

"What?"

"We busted him a dozen years ago on hacking and financial fraud charges. Penny-ante stuff on each count, but enough in aggregate to put him away for a couple of decades. We did a deal with him instead. We cut him loose and he kept doing his thing, and we took all the information he brought in and used it to keep tabs on the worst actors in that arena."

"Is that legal?"

"The arrests we've made have all passed constitutional muster, yes."

"That's a worryingly vague response."

"The point, Mr. Valdez, is that when Cooper died, we lost an incredibly important resource into the cryptocurrency sector. And about his death, we know two things for sure. One, that Cooper wasn't the suicidal type. Two, that Mason Schilling was there when his death happened. And since we know the first, we want to know more about the second. I'm telling you this so you understand how much of a priority it is for us to talk to your friend."

"You said you were investigating a potential murder," I said. "So you think Mason *did* do it."

"We think that whatever Mr. Schilling was doing the night Cooper died, he was doing in an unofficial capacity, outside the color of the law and the remit of his dispatching license," Liu said.

"So, *murder*," I pressed.

"We also think it's possible that the culpability for events may pass through Mr. Schilling to other parties," Liu continued. "Or could, depending on cooperation. Which is why I said to you, truthfully, that we're interested in your friend as a material witness. And we want to find him, obviously, before others do. Or perhaps more accurately, given Mr. Schilling's recent activities on the Expressway, before they find him *again*."

"And you're telling me all this why?" I asked.

"Because I'm hoping you'll see that it's in his interest to come to us."

"Mason is not exactly the kind to help authorities."

"I'm hoping you'll convince him."

"This supposes he'll contact me in any way."

"As I understand it, he asked to see you before he was dispatched. I talked to your colleague Ella Cross at the hospital. That's what she said."

"That was before the dispatch."

"He might contact you after."

"Or you could just pick him up at his home."

"He didn't show up there."

"How do you know?"

"We were there," Liu said. "And we weren't the only ones. Chicago Police rolled up, too. And some other folks who drove off when one of our people started checking plates. Your friend is popular with an interesting collection of people, Mr. Valdez."

"That's Mason," I said. I finished my ice cream and ducked back into Zooabaloo to dispose of the cup and spoon.

"You wouldn't happen to know where he might have reappeared?" Liu asked me, once I was back on the street.

"The dispatched go to where they feel safe," I said. "That's usually their home."

"Not in this case."

"Well, it was being watched by the FBI, the CPD, and various other people. You understand why he might have wound up somewhere else."

"I get why, I just don't know where. I was hoping you might."

"Mason didn't leave me a list," I said. "Is there anything else, Agent Liu?"

"You have no idea where he is, Mr. Valdez?"

"Agent Liu, if there is one thing I'm sure of, it's that even if I *did* know where he was, the very last thing he would want is for me tell the FBI about it."

"So that's a no."

"That's a 'thank you for walking to get ice cream with me,' actually. And any other questions you might have, we can do more formally, with lawyers."

"Got it."

"Lovely to meet you," I said, turning to go.

"I'll walk with you."

"I don't need the escort."

"It's not that," Liu said. "I parked on your street."

I waited for Liu to drive away before going back to the apartment.

Mason was gone.

He left a note:

I took sweats, shoes and some money. I'll pay you back. Thanks for the help. Sorry for the trouble. Burn this note.

Money? I thought, and then went to my bedroom closet, where my safe was.

It was open and three thousand of my five-thousand-dollar stash was gone.

"How the fuck did he know my combination?" I said out loud, to no one in particular.

FIVE

I was in line at Stan's Donuts the next morning when I got an alert on my phone that someone had opened the door to my apartment. My expatriate friend, who had break-ins before I sublet his place, had installed sensors on the doors and windows and used a couple of Echo Shows as surveillance cameras. I took over the sensors when I moved in.

I'd never had a problem with break-ins, but I noticed the sensors tended to go off when birds accidentally hit a window. Plus there was a chance that Mason might have come back to the apartment. I hadn't given him a key, but then, a man who could break into my personal safe probably wouldn't have a problem with the door. I opened up the Alexa app to look at the inside of my apartment.

There were two people in it, neither of whom was Mason.

"Your order?" the lady at Stan's counter asked me.

"What?" I said, and then suddenly remembered where I was. "Sorry, I was watching people breaking into my apartment."

"Got it. Half-dozen assortment, to go?"

"Please." I stepped aside and called Nona Langdon. "Do you have any units by my apartment?" I asked her as soon as she picked up.

"Tony, I'm not a dispatcher," Langdon said. "Either your kind or the kind who sends police cars to people's homes. Have you tried 911?"

"I thought you would be faster. There are a couple of people in my apartment right now."

"Are you there? Are you in danger?" Langdon's voice, despite her previous attitude, had become concerned.

"I'm fine, I'm out getting donuts," I said. "I think they were probably waiting for me to leave the apartment to come in."

"Hold on," Langdon said. She moved her phone from her face and yelled at someone. This established to me she was at her precinct house, not out and about. "There's a CPD unit not far from your place," she said a minute later. "It's on its way. How did you know about the break-in?"

"I've got sensors and cameras," I said. "I was watching them when I called you."

"You have them on video? Are you recording it?"

"I can make screenshots."

"Do it and send them to me."

"Will do."

"And stay away from your apartment until you hear from me again."

"All right," I said. Langdon hung up. I looked up and the counter lady had a small box of donuts ready for me. "Thank you," I said, getting out my wallet.

She held up her hand. "On the house this time," she said. "You're having a break-in. You need a karmic balancer."

I smiled behind my mask, got out my wallet anyway, and left a big tip in the tip jar. That's how you do it.

Langdon told me not to come back to the apartment, but I wasn't going to stay away entirely. This was my home, after all. I walked back on North Avenue in the direction of my street, watching the video of the break-in and sending Langdon screenshots as I did so.

The two people in my apartment appeared to be male, appeared to be white, and weren't making that much of an effort to conceal their identities. One of them picked his nose and then ran his finger along one of my counters, which annoyed me almost as much as his breaking into my apartment. I was going to have to disinfect my whole place now.

The two men were clearly looking for something. They were scanning table tops and looking in desk and kitchen drawers. Whatever it was they were look-ing for, they weren't finding it, and it seemed like they were getting more irritated as they went along. At one point one of them, the nose picker, slapped the table the Echo Show was on and appeared to yell something at the other one, who poked his head out of my bed-room. I snapped another screen shot of him to send to Langdon. Honestly, I was surprised he hadn't figured out the Echo might be looking at him; the camera mod-ule wasn't that difficult to see. Clearly he and the other one were focused on their task, whatever it was.

At this point, I paused for a moment on the street to retrieve a lemon pistachio old-fashioned. Surveilling the people who had invaded your apartment was hun-gry work.

I turned the corner onto my street just as the two men exited my apartment, one of them—not the nose picker—pulling out a phone as the door closed behind them. I looked up from my own phone and saw the police cruiser down the street, out of the immediate sightlines of my apartment's street-facing windows. Two uniformed cops were lurking, waiting for the two men. I didn't see them come out of the building, but I knew it had happened when the police started moving quickly, yelling.

The nose picker decided to run. He sprinted past one of the cops and ran down the sidewalk toward me, the cop trailing behind. As he got close to me, I chucked the remainder of my lemon pistachio old-fashioned at his head. He weaved and ducked and threw up his hands in an attempt to deflect the pastry, passing by me as he did so. I took the opportunity to stick out my leg and trip him. He went down, his head nearly connecting with a street planter as he fell. The cop caught up to us, straddled him, and put him in cuffs.

"Dude, you threw a *donut* at me," the man said as the cop hauled him upright.

"Dude, you left a booger in my apartment," I replied. He stared at me as he was led away.

"So, these aren't your usual home invaders," Langdon said to me. We were in my apartment, a couple of hours later. The arresting officers had taken my statement at the time of the arrests; I had given them each a donut in appreciation. Langdon's visit was technically a follow-up contact. I also offered her a remaining donut. She declined.

"There are usual home invaders?" I asked.

"The usual ones are the ones who break in to rob you," Langdon said. "There is an economic interest, if you want to put it that way. Or they're looking for prescription drugs. But you don't have anything missing."

"No," I agreed. A quick look around the place established that nothing had been taken. The only items missing were the ones Mason took—the sweats, the running shoes, and the cash.

"And you don't have any drugs in the apartment?" Langdon asked.

I gave her a look. "I have some Advil," I said. "Maybe some expired Claritin."

"It's not an entirely unreasonable question," Langdon said.

"If you say so."

"They were here for a pretty long time not to take anything," Langdon said, continuing. "And the screen shots you sent me had them looking through your drawers and possessions. They were looking *for* something."

"It looked that way to me, too," I said.

"Probably not expired Claritin."

"Probably not."

"And you have no personal connection to the two men who were in your apartment?"

"I don't even know who they are," I said. "I don't think I do, anyway."

Langdon nodded at this, pulled out her phone, and opened up the photo app to show me a picture. "This one is Dominick Hawking." She flipped the photo to the other man. "This is Cody Williamson." Both of the men were late twenties to early thirties, both visually inter-changeable with millions of other dudes of their age and physical type. "Ring any bells?"

"Not at all," I said.

"You ever dispatch either of these two?"

"Not that I know of, no," I said. "And it's unusual for someone we dispatch to come for us anyway. Most people we dispatch are happy to be back."

"You haven't run across either them anywhere else? Pissed off one of them in a bar, stole a parking space from one of them, or anything like that?"

"I don't spend a lot of time in bars, and I take the El and rideshares."

"No connection at all."

"Not that I'm aware of."

"Well, then, here's a thing," Langdon said. "You don't have a connection to them. But they have a connection to you."

I furrowed my brow at this. "How?"

"Hawking and Williamson are not exactly career criminals. They have no criminal records at all, except for a DUI Williamson got when he was in college, for which he got community service."

"Community service for a DUI?"

"He comes from a prominent family in North Carolina and the DUI was when he was at Duke. He drove his Jeep up a rival fraternity's front porch. Injured a couple of them doing it, one of them seriously. I'm guessing strings were pulled."

"Must be nice," I said.

"Hawking and Williamson both have tech jobs here in town at SynseMem. You know of it?"

"No."

"It has something to do with haptics software. Every time it feels like you're pressing a button on a touch screen, that's them, or at least some software they licensed to someone else. The CEO of SynseMem is a guy named Michel Cadieux."

"I don't know him."

"No reason why you should, you don't run in the same circles. And Cadieux isn't always here anyway. He splits time between here and Lyon, where SynseMem's other main office is. But he's in town now, and he was on the phone with Hawking when he was arrested."

"He told you that?"

"Neither he nor Williamson has told us anything. They lawyered up the second we put them in the back of the car."

"Then how do you know?"

Langdon smiled. "You'll love this. When I say phone, I mean to say Hawking was talking to Cadieux on an encrypted communication app on his phone. Totally secure on both ends; even if we had a warrant we wouldn't be able to get into it. Totally secure app on a phone that Hawking had no security on. Not even a PIN. The arresting officer saw the app screen on the phone and Cadieux's name was right there, big and bold for the world to see."

"You'd think a tech dude would know better," I said.

"Arrogance is a hell of a drug."

"I'm still waiting to hear how they're connected to me."

"Remember Paul Cooper?"

"The dead billionaire."

Langdon nodded. "The dead billionaire who killed himself at that large party of rich people. Well, guess who else was spotted at that party?"

"I'm guessing Michel Cadieux," I said.

"Yes. And your pal Mason Schilling."

"Ah."

"Yes, 'ah,'" Langdon said. "Schilling present at a party where a billionaire allegedly committed suicide. And then a day later he's jumping out of cars. And then a day after that, after you were present at his dispatch, two employees of someone else at the party break into your apartment and look for *something*. A very specific thing."

"Okay, I get the connection now."

Langdon considered me in that way of hers, which made me a little uncomfortable. "Tony, this is where I tell you I think you're holding out on me."

"How so?"

"If people connected to Mason Schilling are looking for something at your place, it suggests that they might've been looking for him. Or some evidence he was at your place."

"They didn't find him there for a reason," I said. "Or evidence he was there."

"Or they were looking for something he might have had on him."

"Then they don't know how dispatching works," I said. "When you come back, you don't bring anything with you that's not a functional part of you. A pacemaker, yes. Rings and clothes and anything else, no. If there was anything he had with him, he left it at the hospital."

"Agreed," Langdon said. "We have his possessions from the hospital. Shredded clothes and a wallet with money, ID, and credit cards. Nothing else."

"There you go." I didn't say anything about Mason's crypto wallet, which was currently burning a hole in my front left jeans pocket, where it had been all this time. I'd been keeping it on me because after Mason broke into my home safe, I figured anything I wanted secure I should probably keep close.

Langdon looked at me like she was going to say something, and then changed her mind to say something else. "I want you to come with me."

I blinked at this. "Excuse me?"

She gave me a look. "I'm not *arresting* you, Tony. I'm on my way to see Michel Cadieux. He's keeping a skeleton staff working at the SynseMem offices rather than from home, so we know he's there. Hawking had disconnected just before we grabbed him. It's possible Cadieux doesn't know he and Williamson were arrested. I want to see what he does when I show up in his office with you in tow."

"You want to shake him up."

"Something like that. Don't worry, I'll make sure you get your usual consulting rates for your time. Just like the old times."

Twenty minutes later we were in an elevator in the pretty, new SynseMem building, straight across from Google's Chicago headquarters, heading up to the sixth floor and the executive suite. Langdon had to flash her badge to get past the ground floor reception; as we got in the elevator I saw the receptionist make a call. We would not be a surprise.

"What do you want me to do?" I asked Langdon, as we rode up.

"I want you to stand there next to me, not saying anything but looking like you know a hell of a lot more than you're letting on," she said. "You know, like you're already doing."

I smiled, and then the elevator opened to the executive floor. We stepped out, just in time for the gunshot that rang through the hallway.

CHAPTER SIX

Langdon immediately pulled her service weapon and yelled for me and the floor's receptionist to get down. When I was on the ground, she tossed me her walkie-talkie.

"Call it in," she said, in a harsh whisper.

"How do I do that?" I asked.

"It's a goddamn walkie-talkie, Tony!"

Before I could respond, someone turned the corner out of the office corridor into the reception area. Langdon trained her weapon on him. He put up his hands but otherwise did not seem alarmed or surprised to have been drawn upon.

"That's not necessary, Detective Langdon," he said.

"There was a gunshot," Langdon said, not dropping her weapon.

"Everything's fine. No one's in danger," the man continued. "I'm Gray Bradley, Michel Cadieux's executive assistant. Our ground floor receptionist led me to understand you wish to speak to him. He's ready for you, if you'll follow me."

Langdon stared at Bradley for another long moment before holstering her weapon. She looked down at me.

"You still want me to call it in?" I asked.

"Shut up and give me my walkie-talkie," she said. I handed it to her, and after she put it in her inside jacket pocket, I took her hand to get up off the floor. "We're ready," Langdon said to Bradley, who motioned us down the corridor.

"What happened?" Langdon asked Bradley as we walked.

"A product demonstration," Bradley replied.

"You have a product that involves discharging a weapon?"

"No, but we do have products that we want to show can still function after a weapon's been discharged into them. The durability of haptic response in extreme situations is a plus. Some of our people were doing a practice for a client presentation. I apologize if it alarmed you."

Langdon looked skeptical but said nothing.

We were escorted not into Cadieux's office but into a conference room next to it. A long table stood in the middle of the room. A large screen took up one of the walls.

"Where is he?" Langdon asked.

Bradley had his phone out. "I'm connecting him now."

"He's not here?"

"Don't worry, our telepresence connection is very good."

"That's not what I meant—" Langdon began, but then the screen popped on and Michel Cadieux's head appeared in it, looking like it belonged on a giant.

"Detective Langdon, Michel Cadieux," Bradley said, motioning to the screen. "Michel, this is Detective Nona Langdon of the Chicago Police Department." He turned to me. "And this is—"

"I'm the guy whose apartment two of your employees broke into this morning," I said to Bradley, and then looked at Cadieux's image. "But you can call me Tony."

"I'm shocked to hear this," Cadieux said.

"Are you?" I asked.

"Mr. Cadieux," Langdon said, "before we go any further, where are you?"

"I'm at home, Detective Langdon."

"At home, here in Chicago."

"No. In Lyon."

"Lyon as in France."

Cadieux smiled. "There may be other places called Lyon, Detective, but allow me some chauvinism when I say I would never live in those places."

"You were in Chicago less than two days ago, and now you are in France."

"Yes."

"At home."

"Yes."

"Suddenly."

"I wasn't aware, Detective, that there were any rules against international travel at the moment. Maybe in the pandemic, but those days are thankfully past. I assure you I've broken no laws or regulations in returning to my home." Cadieux cocked his head. "But this isn't why we are talking today, am I correct?"

I looked at Langdon. She was generally good at presenting a calm demeanor to the world, and I think someone who didn't know her would find the expression on her face to be courteously and professionally blank. I *did* know her, however, and I could see the subtle tension in her neck and jaw. She didn't like being lied to, which is what Cadieux was doing right now, about his departure from Chicago. She was unhappy. And more than unhappy, she was pissed.

But I also knew she wasn't going to let Cadieux see it. And I was right. "That's correct. We're here to ask you why two of your employees broke into this man's apartment this morning."

"Which two employees are these?"

"Dominick Hawking and Cody Williamson."

"Williamson I don't know very well," Cadieux said. "Hawking I do. He's spearheading one of SynseMem's new product initiatives and for that he reports directly to me."

"So you've spoken to him recently."

"Yes, we talked this morning."

"Can you tell me what that conversation was about?"

"He had some deliverables I asked him to update me on."

I arched my eyebrow at this. Langdon caught it. "What 'deliverables' were these, Mr. Cadieux?" Langdon said.

"Relating to the product he's helping to develop for us. Not anything else."

"You know he was calling you while he was still in the apartment he was burgling."

"The call was audio, not video. The only thing I noticed was it ended abruptly."

"That was when he was tackled by the cops," I said.

Cadieux regarded me and then gave a brief nod. "If you say so."

"It didn't seem strange to you that the call ended abruptly?" Langdon asked Cadieux.

"No," Cadieux said. "I use the HowlRound app for secure communications. I'm one of the angel investors for it. I'm beta testing the next iteration, which means I'm using a pre-release version that still has a lot of bugs in it. It drops calls all the time. I assumed Dom would just get back to me."

"He's going to have difficulty doing that from jail," I suggested.

"I'm curious to know how you learned he was speaking to me at all," Cadieux said to Langdon, ignoring me. "The call was meant to be secure. I may have to file a bug report."

"Your employee left his phone wide open to searching," Langdon said. "No passwords or PINs. We saw the call log on his screen."

Cadieux threw up his hands. "This is the problem with security. Humans."

"We didn't mind," Langdon observed.

"No, of course *you* wouldn't. His failure makes your job easier."

"Mr. Cadieux, just to be clear, you're telling us unequivocally that you have no idea why your two employees were burglarizing an apartment and calling you as they were doing it."

"As I said, I was speaking to Dom about an unrelated matter. I don't know why he decided to do it while he was in"—he pointed at me and paused to remember my name—"Tony's apartment. And I don't know why they decided to enter his apartment at all. It's inexplicable to me."

"I'm confused, too," I assured him.

"Although SynseMem has no responsibility for our employees' conduct outside of the office, I do apologize to you, on behalf of the company."

"Thank you," I said. "That means a lot to me."

I'm not sure Cadieux caught the sarcasm. He turned his attention back to Langdon. "Anything else, Detective?"

"Unrelated to the break-in, I understand you were at a gathering the other night. Here in Chicago."

"Yes," Cadieux said. "At Gabrielle's. That's Gabrielle Friedkin."

"I know who she is," Langdon assured him.

"I thought it was meant to be a small group of friends, but it turned out to be rather more crowded than that. I wasn't pleased with that fact." He motioned at his surroundings. "I was looking forward to a quiet evening with friends."

"You've heard about Paul Cooper's death."

"I have. It's tragic."

"Are you friends with Cooper? Were you, I mean," Langdon amended.

"We were friendly, but not friends," Cadieux said. "At a certain social stratum, everyone knows each other and it makes sense to be friendly. But I wouldn't say he would be my first pick to socialize with."

"Why not?" I asked.

"Are you friends with everyone you meet? Some people are just not *your* people. They may be otherwise fine. But they're not for you."

"And yet you were both in the same place," I said.

"There were a lot of people there, as I said."

"You also said you expected fewer people," Langdon said, cutting in.

"We were both there at Gabrielle's invitation," Cadieux said.

"Is there a reason she would want you both there?" Langdon said.

"Gabrielle likes a mix of people at her parties."

"Two tech billionaires counts as a mix?" I asked.

"We're both in tech, but arrived at success differently," Cadieux said. "Paul came from almost nothing. I started my company from scratch, but my family's been prominent here in Lyon for centuries. And Gabrielle, you could say, is somewhere in the middle."

Langdon and I briefly glanced at each other but said nothing. If Chicago could be said to have old money, the Friedkins would be among the oldest. At one point, the family owned probably half of the Gold Coast and a third of the Loop. Those percentages had come down over the decades, but the Friedkins' fortunes hadn't. One of the many Friedkin cousins was currently running for governor.

"So you have no idea why Cooper might have shot himself?" Langdon asked.

"I don't," Cadieux said. "How awful. He was so young."

"And the presence of a dispatcher at the party is not something you knew about," I said.

"A dispatcher?" Cadieux furrowed his brow. "I don't recall meeting one."

"That's odd," I said. "The dispatcher remembers you."

Cadieux looked suddenly uncomfortable. "Yes. Well. I am not exactly *unknown*, am I?"

"No, I suppose not."

Cadieux looked at Langdon. "What's the disposition of my employees?"

"They're still in custody. Tony here will be pressing charges, so it might take a day or two for them to be arraigned. If they post bail, at that point they'll be out, otherwise they'll continue to be guests of the City of Chicago. And how about you, Mr. Cadieux? When can we expect you back in our borders?"

"I regret to say I'll have to be here in France for the foreseeable future," Cadieux said. "I have some family business that needs to be attended to here. Best to stay put."

"Indeed," Langdon said, dryly.

"And now I'm afraid I must go. Speaking of family, I have an obligation to them this evening. If you have any other questions, Gray here will be more than happy to assist you, or if necessary, SynseMem's general counsel can be at your disposal." He nodded at Langdon. "Detective." He looked at me. "Tony." He disconnected.

Langdon turned to Gray Bradley after the screen went blank. "Now, Mr. Bradley, do you want to tell me what *actually* happened?"

Bradley smiled politely. "I'm afraid I don't know what you mean, Detective Langdon. And even if I did, I'd have to refer you to the company's lawyers."

"You understand that if we find any discrepancies in what Cadieux has told us, it's not his ass that's on the line, it's yours," Langdon said. "He's in France and he's a billionaire. You're neither of these things. His troubles don't have to be your troubles."

"I appreciate your concern for me, Detective. Thank you." He motioned with his hand toward the conference room door. "Shall we?"

As we exited I glanced down the hall, past a custodial cart set up in front of Cadieux's office, to the sign signifying a lavatory. "I'm going to borrow your bathroom for moment," I said to Bradley. "I can find my way back to the reception area when I'm done. See you there in a minute." Langdon nodded and started walking with Bradley, talking to him as she did.

I found the men's room, did my business, washed up and walked out, checking my email along the way. I was so engrossed that I bumped into the custodial cart, which sent my phone tumbling into its trash can.

I groaned at this and peeked into Cadieux's office. "I'm an idiot and just dropped my phone into your trash," I said to the custodian, when I located him in the room. "Do you mind if I dig it out?"

"I can do it for you," he said.

"Nah, that's fine. It's not that far in."

The custodian shrugged. "Help yourself." I nodded and dug into the trash to fish it out. It was further down than I had said. It took me a moment to extract it.

"I was worried you fell in," Langdon said when I came out to the reception area, where she was still talking with Bradley.

"I dropped my phone," I said. "I don't want to talk about it."

The elevator arrived. We said our goodbyes to Bradley and rode the elevator in silence.

"All right, let's talk about this bullshit," Langdon said when we were back out on the street.

"Well, Gray Bradley shot his boss, for one," I said. "Cadieux knew the burglary at my place went bad and was waiting to see if it would come back to him. When we showed up, Bradley blew Cadieux's brains out in his office. He blinked back into existence in France, which doesn't extradite anyone for anything, ever."

Langdon nodded. "Not that we have proof of that."

"Except for the divot in the wall of Cadieux's office, put there by a gun," I said. "Which I saw when I peeked in on the way back from the bathroom."

"I knew you didn't have to pee," Langdon said.

"No, I did have to pee," I said. "But I could've waited."

Langdon offered the briefest of smiles at this, then became serious. "If you're Cadieux, you don't risk dying to get away—unless you think you're in trouble."

"Yeah," I agreed. "And he's convinced he's out of it now because he's in France. Or he was convinced, until I mentioned Mason."

"Which, by the way, wasn't a thing you mentioned to me before, Tony."

"That's because I made it up," I said. "I was just curious what he would do."

"What he did was get off the call as soon as possible after that," Langdon said.

"And tell us to speak to his company lawyers from now on. Which was a turnaround from offering Gabrielle Friedkin up to us willingly. I wonder if he's regretting that now."

"We already knew it was her place," Langdon said.

"Have you talked to her?"

"We're trying to schedule an interview with her and her lawyers now," Langdon said. "This is more complicated than it should be. Any other thoughts?"

"Just one." I reached into my right front jeans pocket and fished out an object and handed it to Langdon.

She took it and looked at it, frowning. "What is this?"

"I'm guessing it's a crypto wallet," I said, as if I had known what that was before Mason had told me. "Probably encrypted. I found it in the trash can when I accidentally dropped my phone into it and had to fish it out."

"'Accidentally,' dropped it, huh."

"What can I say, I'm clumsy."

"I'm not sure it's admissible," Langdon said. "I obtained it without a search warrant."

"You didn't obtain it. I did."

"You were with me on police business."

"It had already been thrown away."

"But it was still inside the premises," Langdon said. "My point is that whatever this is, I don't know that I can use it. I don't even know why it's relevant in the first place."

"Because Mason had one like it on him," I said.

Langdon frowned. "It wasn't among his possessions at the hospital."

"I'm aware of that."

"Remember when I said I had a feeling you were holding out on me? I want you to know I'm feeling it again. Right now. Very much."

"I understand that," I said. "Look. Mason didn't have enough time to tell me everything that happened or how he was involved. Wherever he is right now, he's still in danger. And now he's managed to drag me into it as well. I'm worried about my friend and I'm worried about me. I'm sorry I haven't been perfectly honest with you. But if you're willing to put that aside for right now, I think we can figure this thing out."

"You're going to be totally honest with me now?"

"I'm going to be *more* honest with you."

"Tony," Langdon warned.

"Trust me a little," I said.

"I don't, right now."

"I get that. But trust me anyway."

"Fine," Langdon said after a minute. "Then what do we do right now?"

"I want you to release Cody Williamson," I said.

"The guy who robbed your apartment."

"That's the one."

"Why?"

"Because from what Cadieux told us, he's probably the one who got dragged into this by him and Hawking," I said. "And I'm betting that's going to make it easier to convince him to drag himself out of it."

SEVEN

Cody Williamson lived in Wrigleyville, which is a favorite neighborhood for bros and former fraternity brothers, but we are who we are, I suppose. I caught up with him after my shift at the hospital, which had been a success in that I managed to convince two families not to dispatch their loved ones. They would've ended up right back at the hospital, because they were already too ill. We take our victories where we can.

Langdon let me know just before the end of my shift that Williamson was out on his own recognizance; I took a cab to Wrigleyville and waited. Not at his apartment— that would have been a little much—but at a liquor store on his corner. I figured he'd make a beeline there once he was sprung.

I didn't have long to wait. About a half hour after I arrived, Williamson turned the corner onto Clark and immediately entered the liquor store. I positioned myself near the door for when he came out, mask off.

Which he did a couple of minutes later, carrying a six-pack of cans from a hipster microbrewery, one of which he had already cracked open and was taking a swig from as he exited. As such, it took him a second to recognize that someone was standing directly in front of him, and another second to recognize who that someone was. He froze, mid-swallow.

"Please don't spit your beer out at me," I said.

Williamson swallowed with visible effort and stared at me, uncertain.

"It's too late to run," I told him. "I already know you know who I am."

"What do you want?" Williamson asked.

"I just want to talk."

Williamson smirked at this. "I know you think I'm stupid, but I'm not that stupid."

"You don't want to talk?"

"You can talk to my lawyer, if that's what you want."

"Okay, then, how about this." I pulled Mason's crypto wallet out of my pocket and showed it to Williamson. "I talk and you listen."

Williamson didn't say anything but his eyes widened. I smiled. "I thought so," I said, and put the vault in my pocket. I motioned to Williamson. "You're blocking the store entrance. Let's walk." We headed down his street.

"What now?" Williamson asked after a moment.

"Like I said, I talk and you listen. Look, Cody, I know why you and your friend broke into my apartment. You didn't do it because you two were looking for cheap thrills on a weekday morning. You were doing it because you were told to do it. You were told to do it because someone, probably your boss, wanted you to get the thing I just showed you."

"Do you know what's on it?" Williamson asked.

"I have no idea," I said, which was not true, but Williamson didn't need to know that. "And honestly, I don't care. Have you ever heard of a MacGuffin?"

"A what?"

"A MacGuffin. It's the thing in a movie that everybody's trying to get. What it is isn't important, it's just the thing that drives the action." I patted my pocket. "As far as I'm concerned, this is a MacGuffin. Lots of people seem to want it, and are willing to do stupid things for it. Or in your case, let their underlings do stupid things for it. You know your boss fled, right?"

Williamson stopped. "What?"

"He's in France."

"That's not possible."

"It's possible if you travel by bullet," I said.

It took Williamson a minute to figure out what that meant. "I should really stop talking to you," he said, and started walking again toward his apartment building a few doors away.

"I'm going to drop charges against you," I told him as he walked away.

He stopped walking again, waiting.

"You're being left on the hook by the boss who told you to break into my apartment," I said. "Even if you tried to pin it on him, he's going to find a way to get out of it, and even if we found a way to charge him with it, he's not going to get extradited for it. It's all on you and your pal."

Williamson turned. "Why would you drop the charges?"

"You don't think I would do it out of the kindness of my own heart?"

"No, not really."

"Fair," I said. I patted my pocket again. "Your boss wants this thing really bad. Bad enough to get you to break into my home for it. All right, fine. He can have it. And you can give it to him."

"You're just going to give it to me?"

"Of course not. Your boss is going to pay me for it. Then I'll give it to you."

"Pay you for it."

"Sure," I said. "We meet up, you give me a bag of money, I give you the MacGuffin, charges dropped, everyone's happy."

"How much money?"

It occurred to me that I hadn't actually thought about how much money to ask for. I went for the first number I could think of. "I want three point one four million dollars."

Williamson thought about this for a second. "You want pi million dollars."

"Yes," I said.

"Why pi?"

"It's a nice round number."

"It's literally not."

"Then let's just say that it's enough to solve a lot of my personal problems," I said.

"It's a lot of money."

"Your boss is worth two and a half billion dollars. His whole family is worth ten times that. I checked earlier today. Three million dollars to him is like a hundred bucks to you or me. He can swing it."

"If you say so."

"Ask him," I said. "The worst he can say is no."

"What happens to me if he says no?"

"Prove to me you actually asked, and I'll still drop the charges. But I need proof that you asked."

"Like what?"

"I'll let you figure that out," I said, and patted my pocket one more time. "But I would hurry. I'm guessing your boss isn't the only party interested in this MacGuffin." I took out my wallet and retrieved a business card with my cell number on it. "For when your boss is ready to make a deal."

Williamson stared at my pocket, then at me. Then he took the card, drank another swig of his craft beer in a can, and walked away, for good this time.

"You actually called it a MacGuffin," Langdon said. We were walking in my neighborhood and eating donuts from Stan's. I paid for them this time.

"It's what it is," I said.

"Except that it's not," Langdon pointed out. "It's a real thing, not an imaginary plot device."

"Well, sort of." I reached into my pocket with the hand that was not holding the donut and produced the item. "This is just something I had lying around the apartment. So it really *is* a MacGuffin."

Langdon held out her own non-donut-bearing hand. "Let me see that."

I handed it to her. "I guessed that Williamson was told what to look for but wasn't given a picture of it. So this would work just as well."

"And in showing this to him, you confirmed it was what he and Hawking were looking for."

"Right."

"So where is the *actual* thing?" Langdon asked.

"I saw it in Mason's hand," I said. "I went out and bought the closest thing to what I remember it looking like."

"You're telling me you don't have it."

"I don't have it, no," I said. I held out my hand.

Langdon gave the drive back to me. "It was in his hand when he was dispatched and then it disappeared, but everything else of his stayed behind," she said. "You know how suspicious that is."

"It doesn't have to be suspicious. It was in his hand when he was dispatched. It could've dropped to the floor. He was in the ER. It's not exactly a sedate environment. It could've been accidentally kicked under a crash cart or something."

Langdon grunted but didn't say anything. She bit into her donut.

"Speaking of which, any news on Mason?" I asked, putting the drive back into my pocket.

Langdon shook her head. "Not at home, no activity on his online accounts, and no one who knows him has seen him." She grimaced. "That's not accurate. No one who knows him wants to admit to having seen him, and we haven't caught anyone in obvious lies. Not that there were many friends to canvass, Tony. Schilling's not a very popular guy."

"Mason decided a while ago he liked having business associates more than he liked having friends," I said.

"And which are you?"

"I'm a little of both," I admitted. "One more than the other, depending on circumstances."

"He asked for you when he was dying," Langdon pointed out. "That puts you on one end of the spectrum more than the other."

"Don't be so sure. If Mason's lawyer was there, I'm pretty sure he'd be the one called over."

"Incidentally, Mason's lawyer was totally unhelpful."

"I imagine Mason pays his lawyer very well to be that way to the police," I said. "Anything else on Michel Cadieux?"

"No, the SynseMem legal people are being helpfully unhelpful, speaking of lawyers. The crypto wallet thing you pulled out of the trash is equally unhelpful. It's got a fingerprint scanner on it. Our tech people put it into a computer and it won't even let them access a file directory without the right print. They're working on it but they're not optimistic. If Cadieux were still in Chicago, I might be able to get Judge Kuznia to give us a warrant to compel him to open it up, but he's in France so the point is moot."

"Anything else about the party he and Mason were at?"

"We're still piecing that together," Langdon said. "Mostly Gabrielle Friedkin's party pals—old money rich kids and new money arrivals, with some hangers-on. Cadieux was right that she likes a mix of people."

"A mix as long as they're rich," I noted.

Langdon nodded. "There were three billionaires there. Friedkin, Cadieux, and Cooper. One of the witnesses says the three of them might have been talking business at one point."

"I didn't know the Friedkins were into tech. I thought they just owned Chicago."

"Gabrielle recently started a venture capital fund to dip her toe in. It's called Shikaakwa Partners."

I looked at Langdon funny. She caught the look. "It's from the original Native American name for the area."

"That's not appropriative at all," I said.

"It's not the Friedkin family's venture capital fund, either," Langdon continued. "It's hers. She's been recruiting others to be partners. Cadieux is one. Apparently she wants her own money, not just the family's. Which is not to say she's above using family funds to start the thing."

"You know a lot about this."

"I'm a detective, Tony. This is my job. Also, I read an article about it in *Crain's*. It does help explain the party if it was a down-low business event."

I nodded. "It's a lot of money in one room."

"And it *was* in one room," Langdon said. "A couple of the partygoers said that at some point everyone worth ten figures just up and disappeared, along with one other guest."

"Let me guess," I said. "That other guest was Mason."

"That's a good guess, but we think he was there to work, so technically he's staff."

"So who was the other guest?"

"Brennan Tunney."

"Well, shit," I said.

"Speaking of people who are somewhere between friends and business associates," Langdon said.

"We are definitely not friends," I assured her. "And I don't have business with him if I can avoid it."

"But you *do* have business with him."

"Not recently," I said. "Do you know why he was there? He's not young. Or in tech. Or a billionaire. He's probably just a common several-hundred-millionaire."

"Brennan Tunney definitely doesn't talk to us," Langdon said. "*You* might ask him, though."

"Pass. What about Paul Cooper?"

"Still dead. Currently in the morgue. The body's due to be released to the family today. Maybe. There's some confusion about that."

"What do you mean?"

She shook her head. "Cooper's mother and father have competing claims to the body. Apparently she wants him buried and he wants him cremated. Both hate each other's guts and are throwing lawyers at each other about it."

"That's nice."

"It gets better," Langdon said. "Cooper died without a will. All his stock and the controlling interest in MoreCoinz are now intestate. Cooper's entire family—parents and siblings—are already fighting over it."

"How does a billionaire die without a will?" I asked.

"Just because you're a billionaire doesn't mean you're smart," Langdon said. "Cooper was twenty-nine. He obviously didn't think he was going to die anytime soon. No one does when they're twenty-nine."

"No one thinks they are going to die soon, no matter what age they are," I said. "It's always a surprise."

There was a buzz in my pocket. I switched the donut to the other hand and retrieved my phone to read the text there. I smiled.

"What is it?" Langdon asked.

I showed her the phone. "We're on for noon tomorrow," I said. "Williamson got my pi money."

EIGHT

I sneezed as we turned onto Washington Street.

"Bless you," Langdon said from the driver's seat. She was taking me to my exchange with Williamson.

"Thank you," I said, and fished in my pockets, looking for a tissue, which, unless it had materialized magically in the last few minutes, would not be there.

Langdon noticed my struggles. "Glove compartment," she said.

"Thank you," I said again, pawing open the compartment.

"Hay fever?" she asked.

"Not unless I've been afflicted overnight." I found the little plastic-wrapped packet of tissues and pulled one out. "Sometimes you just have to sneeze, you know?" I placed the packet back, closed the glove compartment, blew my nose in the extracted tissue, and then looked for where to dispose of the used wad.

"That goes into your pocket," Langdon said.

"I'm going to get mucus all over the USB drive," I warned, stuffing the tissue into my pocket.

"Not my problem."

"Not worried about tainting the chain of evidence?"

"That's not what that means, Tony."

"I'm not so sure."

"I'm more worried about this exchange," she said. "I don't like the location."

"You don't like the Bean?" I asked.

"One, it's called the Cloud Gate, and two, no."

"No one in the history of the Bean has ever called it the Cloud Gate," I said.

"That's its name."

"Doesn't matter. If the artist wanted it to be called something other than the Bean, he should've made it look like something other than a huge, mirrored bean. And what's wrong with the location?"

"It's wide open."

"I thought that was the point," I said. "Wide open, massively public location where neither of us is likely to get away with murdering the other to get what they're carrying before we make the exchange. And then CPD comes at Williamson from every direction as he walks away."

"I'm not saying it doesn't make sense," Langdon said. "I'm saying I don't like it."

"I appreciate your concern for my well-being."

"I'm not worried about your well-being. I'm worried that a twenty-four-year-old is going to juke past all my people and sprint down Michigan and make us look like fools."

"Oh," I said.

"I'm worried about you, too," Langdon added.

"No, no, it's too late for that."

Langdon pulled over just before State Street. "Get out," she said.

"Sorry?"

"I have to park and I don't want to risk Williamson seeing you get out of the car. Walk the rest of the way. We're early anyway."

"How long do you need to park?"

"Don't worry about it, my people are already there. Just make sure that when he walks away, he's got that USB drive on him. And maybe trip him if he decides to run. Again."

I smiled and got out of the car.

The Bean was as it always was: crowded with people taking pictures of it and of themselves in it. I scanned to see if I could find Williamson in the crowd and could not. Well, as Langdon said, I was early. I went to the underside of the Bean, just under the omphalos, which is where we'd agreed to meet. I looked up to see my distorted self among the other people, then pulled out my phone and waited.

Williamson showed up at noon, almost on the dot. "Put that away," he said to me about my phone as he walked up.

"I'm not recording you," I said.

"Then you won't mind putting that away."

"Have it your way." I put my phone away and then looked at him critically. "Where is it?" I asked.

"Where is what?"

"Where's my money? Pi million dollars isn't a small amount. I thought you'd be carrying a tote bag."

Williamson held up a USB drive. "It's in here."

"The hell you say."

He actually rolled his eyes at me, the jerk. "Come on, dude. It's access to a crypto escrow account. You know this is how they roll."

"It's not how *I* roll," I said. "I roll with actual physical cash I can touch and smell. No cash, no sale."

"I told him you would say that," Williamson said. "So he gave you tau million dollars as compensation."

"What?"

Williamson smiled. "And here I thought you knew math. Tau? As in, two times pi? Six-point-two-eight million."

"That's a lot more than I asked for."

"You said it yourself, he's a billionaire. He can afford it. And he really wants what you have. Speaking of which, show it to me."

I held up the USB drive I'd had in my pocket.

"How do I know it's the real one?" Williamson asked.

"How do I know there's tau million dollars in *your* drive?"

"There might be more; that's just what the crypto in the wallet was worth when he signed off on it."

"And it might be less, if he or one of his billionaire pals sent out a snarky tweet about that particular coin. Or there might be none, because you're scamming me. See, this is why I wanted cash."

"Well, what I have is what I have," Williamson said. "Take it or don't."

"Same here," I said, and held out the drive.

Williamson appeared to think about it for a minute, weighing his options, then walked up to me, holding out his own drive. We both grabbed the other simultaneously, and let go of the ones we held. Williamson stared for a moment at the one he now had in his hand, and then looked at me. "Let's never do this again," he said.

"Suits me. Which direction you want to go?"

He pointed east. I nodded and headed out from under the Bean, walking toward Michigan Avenue. Only to be stopped immediately by someone walking up to me, flashing an ID. "Tony Valdez," he said. "Agent Andrew Liu, Federal Bureau of Investigation."

"We've met." I noticed that I was being surrounded by other potential FBI agents.

"So we have. Tony, I'm placing you under arrest."

I held up the USB drive I had in my hand. "Because of this?"

"For starters."

"Cody Williamson working for you?"

"Yes, he is," Liu said.

"Unbelievable."

"Believe it. You have the right to remain silent," he began, then stopped. "Why are you laughing?"

"Look over there," I said, pointing to my left.

Liu looked at me suspiciously and then looked to my left, where Cody Williamson was being led away in handcuffs by the Chicago Police Department, while other Bean visitors snapped photos of the event.

As he looked, Nona Langdon turned in our direction and saw the FBI surrounding me. She stopped and her fellow police stopped with her.

"What the actual hell is going on here?" she said, in a deeply irritated tone of voice.

"Tell me your interest in Cody," Liu asked Langdon, as we all sat in a conference room in the FBI's Chicago field office—an aggressively bland chunk of government architecture west of the Loop. We had regrouped there after it was decided that Liu and Langdon yelling at each other about jurisdiction and cooperating witnesses while passers-by were snapping pictures and taking video wasn't a good look. Now we were all staring at each other across a conference table, me and Langdon on one side, Liu and Williamson on the other.

"He's a petty criminal, for starters," Langdon said.

Liu smiled. "You're speaking of his breaking and entering into Mr. Valdez's apartment. He was working for us when he did that."

"The FBI signed off on burglary?" I asked.

"No, but we knew the burglary was going to happen, and why. Cody was invited to participate by Hawking at the instigation of Cadieux, and we wanted what they were looking for."

I pointed to my USB drive on the table. "That."

"Yes, that. Evidence you had been in contact with Mason Schilling and he passed it along to you."

"Which matters why?" Langdon asked.

"It matters because that drive unlocks evidence of various crimes we're interested in, including money laundering, insider trading, and other financial-related activities, on the part of Cadieux and several others." He looked over at me. "And because, as I explained to Mr. Valdez when I met him earlier this week, we think his friend Mason is involved in the death of Paul Cooper in some way."

"That would be Paul Cooper the billionaire," Langdon said.

"Yes."

"Who was also working for you, along with Mr. Williamson here."

"Yes," Liu said. "Well. The two of them didn't know each other. We've had Cadieux under investigation for a while."

"For what?"

"For other things, and I'll leave it at that."

"You have a lot of snitches working for you," Langdon observed.

"We're the FBI, Detective Langdon. Cultivating snitches is our pastime." Liu tapped my USB stick. "Sometimes it pays off."

"Except it's not the drive you're looking for," I said. "I bought that at Jewel." I turned to Williamson. "Sorry."

"I mean, there's not six million in my USB drive, either," Williamson said.

"We figured you'd try to scam Cody," Liu said. "Which is why while we were arresting you, we were also searching your condo."

I blinked. "What?"

"Did you bother to get a warrant this time?" Langdon asked.

"I'll have it available for Tony's perusal before he leaves," Liu assured her. He turned his attention to me. "And you should know we already found another crypto wallet."

I nodded. "Of course you did. A regular USB stick, anyway." I pointed to the USB drive on the table. "That came in a two-pack."

Liu's brow furrowed. "But you knew to show Cody a USB drive."

"Sure," I said. "I already told Detective Langdon I saw Mason holding one at the hospital. Then he was dispatched and it went missing afterward. You can search my apartment all you like; you're not going to find it there."

Liu looked at me critically. I understood the glance, stood up, and emptied my pockets onto the desk. There were my wallet, phone, pocket change, a dirty kleenex, and lint. "Happy?" I asked when I was done.

"Not really," Liu admitted.

"I don't have it," I repeated. "Search everything I have. You won't find it."

Liu looked over to Langdon. "And you agree with this?"

Langdon started to speak and then stopped.

"Allow me to interpret that," I said, filling in the sudden gap. "The detective thinks I've been hiding something from her about what happened when Mason was dispatched, but she has yet to find anything to contradict what I've told her."

"That accurate?" Liu asked Langdon.

Langdon shot me a look. "I wouldn't have characterized it that way to you," she said to Liu.

"So that's a yes. But you're still working with this character." Liu jabbed a thumb in my direction.

"We have a history," Langdon said. Then she nodded in the direction of Williamson. "What's your excuse for him?"

"His dad went to Vanderbilt with the deputy director. We pulled strings to keep him out of jail when he was in college. He's been an ear for us in tech since. I inherited him when he came to Chicago. He's been marginally useful."

"I'm *right* here," Williamson said to Liu.

"I said what I said," Liu replied blandly.

"Were you there when he burglarized my apartment?" I asked.

"We had someone monitoring. But we needed him to deliver Schilling's crypto wallet to Cadieux. He was the get, not Hawking, and not just the wallet itself. We needed proof Cadieux was fully engaged in the various things we were investigating. Cooper was helping us get that, but then he wound up dead."

"So whatever it is that's going on, Cadieux is at the heart of it," Langdon said.

Liu shook his head. "Not at the heart of it. A participant, yes. But there are bigger fish."

"Bigger than a billionaire."

"There are bigger billionaires involved."

"Okay," Langdon said. "Tell me who."

"Why?"

"Cooperation can be helpful. I have a suspicious death and a missing person. You have whatever it is you're investigating. And thanks to these two"—she waved at me and Williamson—"we know they're related." Langdon's phone buzzed; she took it out to check the message.

"I think we need more than that," Liu said. "We got our investigations tangled up, I admit that. What happened at the Bean was embarrassing."

"I told you no one calls it the Cloud Gate," I said to Langdon. She ignored me.

"Since both Valdez and Cody here were working with law enforcement, I suggest we agree not to pursue any criminal charges against either," Liu continued, ignoring my outburst. "We can let our press offices handle the rest of the fallout from here. But, Detective Langdon, unless you have some other reason for us to cooperate, I think the FBI is happy to continue to go it alone."

Langdon looked up from her phone. "You're still interested in Paul Cooper, right?"

"What about him?"

"He's missing."

"He's not missing. He's dead."

"He's dead *and* he's missing," Langdon said, and turned her phone around for Liu to look at her message. "Someone just walked into the Cook County Medical Examiner's office and rolled off with the body."

"What?" Liu leaned forward to look at the message.

Langdon pulled her phone back. "So, are we cooperating now? Or do you want to contact my press office to find out what happened?"

CHAPTER

NINE

I buzzed Langdon up to my apartment from the street and let her know the door was open. She came in and took a look around. "I see the FBI didn't pick up after they turned over your place," she said. She was holding a folder.

"You're not wrong," I said from the kitchen, where I was putting dishes back into cupboards. Everything that had been in a cupboard or drawer was out of it, presumably so the cupboards and drawers could be inspected for secret nooks and crannies where I might hide Mason's crypto wallet. Likewise, everything that could be opened was opened. Nothing had been closed or put back.

"Did they find anything?"

"Not what they were looking for. Although they did paw through my dirty laundry, literally. Agent Liu told me they confiscated the USB drive they found, to test it. I wished him luck with that."

"You didn't put anything on it, I hope."

"It was as blank as the one I traded Williamson for."

"So where did you hide Mason's actual crypto wallet?" Langdon asked.

I glanced over at her. "I see what you're trying to do."

"I just thought I'd check."

"I already told you I don't have it."

"I acknowledge you already told me that," Langdon said.

I motioned to encompass the apartment. "You're welcome to look if you like. I can wait to put everything back until you're done."

"That's not why I'm here."

"Why *are* you here? Not that I don't appreciate seeing you. But after the fiasco of Williamson being an FBI stooge and then you and Agent Liu running off to the medical examiner's office together, I thought I'd been excused from further participation."

"I thought so, too," Langdon admitted. "But then something came up at the ME's, and I wanted to talk to you about it." She waved the folder in her hand.

"What's in the folder?" I asked.

"A picture of the people who picked up Paul Cooper's body."

"How did *that* happen anyway?" I said. "I would think the death of a billionaire whiz kid would be something the medical examiner would want to investigate. And keep locked down."

"It *was* being investigated, and the medical examiner doing the investigation hadn't released the body yet."

"So how was the body released?"

"A release order was forged and put into the system," Langdon said. "Then our 'bodynappers' showed up with a minivan from the Michaelson Funeral Home. You familiar with it?"

"Why would I be?"

"Your line of work."

"My job is to keep people out of funeral homes, not to put them in one."

"A little family-owned funeral home in River West. Their paperwork had them picking up the body at the request of Cooper's parents."

"I thought the parents were fighting over his body."

"They *are* fighting over his body. Or were, until it went missing. The funeral home paperwork was forged as well. The funeral home director said she knew nothing about it."

"What about her minivan?"

"It was stolen last night. She filed a police report this morning, before Cooper's body was taken. So that checks out, at least."

"That explains the funeral home side of things, but not the medical examiner's side."

"Well, for that I'm guessing our old friends bribery and graft played a part," Langdon said. "We're investigating that now. So is the FBI, for that matter."

"It's nice when law enforcement gets along," I said dryly, then nodded to Langdon's folder. "But you have a lead on the people who took the body."

"Sort of. They showed up wearing masks."

"They were there to pick up a body, so that makes sense."

"Unfortunately it makes it more difficult to identify people," Langdon said. "We have the paperwork they submitted to get the body, but since that's forged, it's not as if that's going to be reliable in any way."

"The paperwork might have fingerprints," I suggested.

"Thank you for telling me my job, Tony," Langdon said. "And no, nothing came up. The security cameras have them wearing gloves through the entire transfer."

"So all you have is a picture of masked men."

"Yes," Langdon said. "But I also have you." She opened the folder, slid the photo out, and put it on top of the short stack of plates I had yet to place back into the cupboard. "Tell me what you see, Tony."

What I saw was a picture taken from the security camera immediately outside the doors of the medical examiner's office, where bodies were brought in and taken back out again. The minivan from the Michaelson Funeral Home was visible, beige with black lettering on the side. It wasn't a hearse; it was strictly for pickup from the medical examiner, which was not usually seen by the family. Two men were rolling out a stretcher with a body on it—Paul Cooper's.

"He shot himself, yes?" I asked Langdon.

"He was shot, at least," she said. "In the chest. Single shot. Pulped his heart, basically."

"And the death's been officially ruled a suicide."

Langdon shook her head. "As I understand it, the ME was leaning toward 'death by misadventure.'" She nodded at the image. "Cooper had a concealed carry license, so he could have a handgun with him. His revolver wasn't registered to him, though. Serial number trace comes up with nothing."

"You could look through his social media to see if he's ever showed it off," I said. "Nerds who have guns tend to display them."

"I'll look into that," Langdon said. "We have his laptop but can't get into because it needs a physical ID, so any pictures on it aren't accessible."

I looked at the corpse in the photo again. "So, the ME doesn't think this is a suicide? Did Cooper *accidentally* put the gun to his chest and pull the trigger?"

"I said the ME was leaning toward death by misadventure, not that it's a final decision. Forget about Cooper for now, Tony. Look at the men carting him off."

I glanced back down at the photo. One of the men I didn't recognize at all. He could have been any of hundreds of thousands of average-looking, slightly bald white men in the city, and that would have been without the mask.

The second man I knew, even with the mask. I knew him very well. He had been in my apartment a few days prior.

And had taken my money.

"Well, shit," I said.

"Say it," Langdon said. "Actually say it. Out loud."

I looked up at her. "That's Mason Schilling."

I had finally gotten the apartment completely picked up when the front door buzzed again. "I'm Ricardo Gomez," a voice said when I answered. "I'm an attorney with a private practice. I have a client who's interested in working with you."

"I'm not doing any private work right now," I said.

"It's not a dispatching job. It's more like consulting."

"It's still private work and I'm not doing any of that."

"The consultation fee includes ten thousand dollars just for taking the meeting."

"What?"

"Look out your window, Mr. Valdez."

I went to the windows facing out to the street and looked down. A man holding a briefcase walked away from the door of the building, stood on the sidewalk, and opened the briefcase. Inside was a whole lot of money.

"That seems excessive," I said when we both returned to the intercom.

"You and I don't disagree," Gomez said. "Call the down payment an expression of good will."

"Nobody's will is that good."

"Then call it a recognition that money talks. Either way, my client very much wants to speak to you. Tonight."

"Who is your client?"

"Someone who can afford to blow ten thousand dollars on a gesture," Gomez said. "And can afford rather more after that."

"Hold, please," I said. I walked away from the intercom, grabbed my phone, and looked up Ricardo Gomez. A LinkedIn listing popped up with a picture that matched the face that had just pointed a briefcase of money at me. Gomez's listing noted he'd gone to Northwestern for undergrad, University of Pennsylvania for law, and his practice was, indeed, boutique and private.

I was, despite everything, curious who the client was. And also, ten thousand dollars was ten thousand dollars.

I masked up, walked down to the front door of the building, opened it, and pointed to the briefcase. "Let me have that," I said.

Gomez handed it over. "I'll be wanting the briefcase back," he said. "It's a Berluti."

"I'm not sure what that means," I admitted.

"It means it's worth almost as much as what's in it."

"Okay. Give me a minute." I closed the door on him, walked the briefcase up to my apartment, and transferred the money into my safe. Then I locked up my apartment and walked back down the stairs to Gomez. "I don't think I would spend that much on a briefcase," I said, returning it to him.

"I didn't," Gomez said. "It's a gift from a client."

"The same client who spends ten thousand dollars on a meeting?"

"Allow me some attorney-client privilege, please, Mr. Valdez." He motioned toward the street. "Shall we?"

As we walked away from my building a vehicle drove up, a black Cadillac Escalade, late model.

I laughed.

"Something funny?" Gomez asked.

"I was wondering what kind of car would show up if I ran the plates on this Escalade," I said.

"I'm not sure what's prompting that comment."

"A friend of mine had a bad experience recently with a car just like this one. In fact, he almost died. Almost."

"Interesting," Gomez said blandly. "Well, Mr. Valdez, let me just say this. If my client wanted to do anything other than talk to you, they wouldn't have had me show up with a stack of bills."

"This implies other options were possibly on the table."

"It does no such thing."

"I'm happy to hear you say that," I said. "But let's stay off the Dan Ryan just in case."

CHAPTER TEN

Our destination was Old Town and a new development called the Fairwood Glen, three towers of luxury apartments grafted onto a location that used to have mixed-income housing. The final tower was breaking ground, or so a billboard informed me as we drove up. I was deposited, along with Gomez, at the front one of the buildings. The billboard looked slightly weathered. The pandemic had stopped a lot of things, which then had difficulty starting up again. The final tower of Fairwood Glen appeared to be one of them.

"There a problem with the last tower?" I asked Gomez, pointing to the aging billboard.

"We had to pause during the pandemic," he said. "Safety concerns, city ordinances, that sort of thing. We're back on track now. We're optimistic the third tower will be finished by the end of the year."

"That's ambitious."

"We're motivated." He motioned me into the lobby. The lobby security apparently recognized Gomez and waved him through to the elevators. Gomez took out a card and swiped it against a panel on the wall; a light above one of the elevator doors lit up, signaling it was the one we were to use.

"Fancy," I said.

"Basic security," Gomez said. "Well, basic for a tower like this. All the residents have a key. It takes them to their floor. If you don't have a key to a floor, the elevator won't let you out there."

"And if you want to visit a neighbor on another floor?"

"That neighbor can give you a one-time clearance. There's a phone app."

"Puts a damper on surprise birthday parties."

"No one likes surprise birthday parties," Gomez said. The elevator door opened and we got in. Aside from an alarm button, there were no other controls.

The elevator deposited us in a smaller private lobby on the thirty-first floor. A security agent there looked at Gomez's ID, typed in both our names and buzzed a door for us. We entered into a massive penthouse apartment. It was dressed out in the modern, clean style that looks great in *Crain's* or *Architectural Digest* but is sterile and uncomfortable in real life.

"Does someone actually live here?" I asked.

"My client does," Gomez said.

"Are they a neat freak?"

"No, but they have staff." He motioned me toward the stairs.

We eventually arrived at a rooftop terrace, complete with pool. By the pool, two middle-aged men stood, very conspicuously not speaking to each other.

"Which one of them is your client?" I asked.

"Neither," Gomez said. "They're my client's meeting after you." He pointed down the terrace. "That's my client there."

A woman was sitting at a low table, reading a book in a manner that could only be described as insouciant. Up until that moment, I hadn't realized that one could, in fact, read or do anything insouciantly; I thought it was only a thing people did in books. And yet here we were.

Gomez led me over to her. She was still engrossed in her book. On the table were a half-full wineglass and a handbag that I was sure, if I looked it up, would be worth at least three times as much as the briefcase Gomez had been so concerned about.

"Tony Valdez—my client, Gabrielle Friedkin," Gomez said as we walked up.

At this, Friedkin finally looked up and smiled at me. "Tony," she said, as if she'd known me all my life, or at least, had known *of* me. "Thank you for accepting my invitation to chat."

"You made a compelling argument," I said.

"I wanted to make sure you knew I valued your time."

"You made me aware of what it's worth, for sure." I nodded to her book. "Interesting reading?"

"This thing?" She flipped it to glance at the title. It was called *Building the Gray City*, by Gary Dorn. "It's supposed to be a history of my family in Chicago. Written by an investigative reporter at the *Tribune*. Used to be at the *Tribune*, anyway. I believe he got laid off when they got purchased by the latest asset management firm. Just as well. It's not very good."

"It's not accurate?"

"No, it's accurate enough. It's just *boring*. Our family is so much more interesting than this." She set the book down on the table, next to her bag. "Now, Tony. Please sit." She motioned to a chair across the low table from her. I sat; Gomez sat as well, catty-corner from both of us.

"This is a nice view," I said, looking at the Chicago skyline.

"It's all right," Friedkin said, not looking at it. "We're hoping whoever buys this penthouse likes it."

"I thought you lived here."

"It's one of my residences, for now. I'll keep it for a few more months and then we'll put it on the market. There's a certain type of high-end buyer for whom it'll be more valuable because they can say they bought the penthouse I used to own."

"An expensive way to make a sale."

"We built the tower," she said. "My personal costs are lower than you think."

"That's nice if you can manage it," I said.

"It's all right," Friedkin said again. "Money and capital are tools, Tony. And at a certain point, actual sums become…transparent. Almost irrelevant."

"I'm not quite there, I have to admit."

"It's the American dream, though, isn't it?" Friedkin opened her arms to encompass the terrace and its view. "Work hard, be smart, and with a little bit of luck, you can have all this." She put her arms down. "Of course, it helps to have a bit of a head start. I'd be a fool not to acknowledge that much. Still, I've done my part to build the family fortune. Am doing my part. I didn't rest on my trust fund."

"All right," I said.

Friedkin smiled. "I take this to mean you want me to get to my point."

"I still don't actually know why I'm here," I acknowledged.

"Let's get down to business, then." Friedkin leaned forward in her chair. "I need your help locating Mason Schilling."

"This is going to be a short meeting, I'm afraid," I said. "I have no idea where he is."

"I didn't say I think you know where he is. I said I need your help finding him."

"If I don't know one, I'm not sure how I can help you with the other."

"Let's just say I have reason to believe you know more than you're willing to admit to the FBI or your friend at the Chicago police."

I looked at her doubtfully. "Are you...spying on me?"

"It's not spying," Gomez cut in. "As part of my practice I keep contacts among law enforcement. Occasionally they tell me things."

"Out of the goodness of their hearts, no doubt."

"That's one way of putting it. I prefer to say I offer a consulting fee for their services. Perfectly legal and above board."

"I'm skeptical."

"The point, Mr. Valdez, is that keeping tabs on you hasn't been all that difficult."

"Especially when you're being arrested at the Bean," Friedkin said. "That little snafu was all over local media this afternoon. I'm surprised you haven't been chased down by reporters the entire day."

"How does all of this convince you I know more about Mason than I'm letting on?"

Friedkin smiled. "It doesn't. Him asking for you in the hospital does."

I looked over at Gomez. "More consultants?"

"You can never have too many," he said.

"He wanted a friend," I said, turning my attention back to Friedkin.

"Tony, I know Mason, a bit. We've had business. If I know anything about him, it's that he doesn't want *friends*. If ever there was a person for whom all relationships were transactional, it's Mason."

"So what was your transaction with him?" I asked.

"Gabrielle," Gomez began.

Friedkin held up her hand but didn't break her gaze at me. "It's all right, Ricardo. It's a fair enough question. Tony, I met Mason at a gathering hosted by another friend. One of my crowd, and I'm sure you know what that means. As part of the evening's festivities he was offering a final destination service. You know what that is, I'd guess."

I nodded. Gomez looked a little lost, so I turned to him. "It's when you intentionally overdose on a drug, usually heroin or fentanyl. It's called a 'final destination' because in the old days it was the sort of trip you wouldn't come back from."

"That sounds…*stupid*," Gomez said.

"It is," I agreed. I turned back to Friedkin. "And your friend had Mason there to supervise."

"That's right. My friend referred to him as the 'death sommelier,' which he thought terribly clever. I don't think Mason cared for the title much. But he did what he was there to do, which was to administer the drugs and make sure the overdoses took, safely and comfortably."

"And did *you* take a trip?" I asked.

Friedkin made a face. "Of course not. I understand the boredom of the indolent rich, Tony. Really, I do. I'm not that bored. I don't play with death for kicks. A one in a thousand chance of it being permanent is too much for me."

I nodded again. "That explains how you met Mason. It doesn't explain why he was at your own party." I caught Gomez's look. "I have my own sources, you know. Even without a consulting fee."

"He was there as a precautionary measure," Friedkin said.

"You're going to have to explain that."

"I already did explain it. The indolent rich find their own fun, Tony. Cocaine in the bathroom. Sex in the spare room. A little light murder in the kitchen with the chef's knives."

"You need to find new friends," I said.

"It's not *everyone*," Friedkin said. "And it's not anything I condone. But from a liability point of view, it's something I have to plan for when I throw a large party."

"Still feels risky," I said.

"Life has risks, Tony. In the grand scheme of things, these are small ones."

I thought of Joe Syzmanski with a tube down his throat and his son and daughter-in-law desperate to do anything for him, and I kept my retort to myself. "But some of your pals knifing the help is a bigger risk," I said instead.

"No one knifes the *help*," Friedkin said, offended.

I cocked my head. "Is that déclassé?"

"Valdez," Gomez said warningly.

"It's not *consensual* that way," Friedkin explained. "It's one thing to ask people to make you food, serve you drinks, and clean up after you and pay them for the service. It's another to ask them to let you literally carve them up for a paycheck. It's not done."

"I assure you it's done," I said.

"Then it's not done by *me*. Or anyone I associate with."

"But enough consensual knifings happen that it makes sense to have a dispatcher on staff for parties, is what you're saying to me."

"It's not all knifings," Friedkin said, and then frowned, perhaps realizing that the sentence that just came out of her mouth would never sound good in any context, ever. "What I'm saying is that at any large party it makes sense to have specialized staff. Caterers for food. Valets for parking. Dispatchers for…misadventures."

"Which you had," I prompted.

Friedkin nodded. "Paul Cooper. I had no idea he'd brought a gun to the party. I had no idea he'd use it on himself. We heard the gunshot. Mason got to him and attempted the dispatch, but it was too late. But that's not all that Mason did."

I furrowed my brow. "What else did Mason do?"

"He robbed Paul's corpse."

ELEVEN

"Excuse me?" I said. "Mason robbed a corpse?"

Gabrielle Friedkin sighed. "Paul wasn't just at the party to enjoy himself. He and I had business, and we had business with each other. I gave him a crypto wallet that stored confidential information. Mason took it off the body after Paul shot himself."

"Why would he do that?"

"I haven't the slightest idea. Maybe he thought it contained cryptocurrency. Paul ran that exchange app."

"You don't do cryptocurrency?" I asked.

"I have a small amount as part of my portfolio," Friedkin said. "But I don't trade it on an *app*."

I smiled at her disgust. "If not crypto, then what?"

"That's confidential," Gomez said. "But I can tell you this much. Just before Paul shot himself, I saw Mason talking to Brennan Tunney at the party."

"What does that have to do with anything?" I asked.

"Perhaps nothing," Gomez said. "And perhaps Brennan and Ms. Friedkin are currently rivals for a significant development in DuPage County, and Mason opportunistically took the drive because he thought it might curry favor with Tunney."

"That's the very definition of a stretch," I said to Gomez.

"Tony, it doesn't matter *why* he took it," Friedkin said. "It matters *that* he took it. He took it, it's mine, and it has confidential information on it that I need back. Mason can't even do anything with it. It's encrypted and only Paul could access it. But even having it out there is a risk I don't want to take."

"Which brings us back to *you*, Mr. Valdez," Gomez said.

"You were with Mason when he was dispatched," Friedkin said. "The police, the FBI, and Michel all believe you're involved. And you do know about the wallet. That's how you tried to entrap Michel's employee. I don't think you have the wallet—"

"Thank you for that," I said.

"—but I don't think you've been entirely honest about what you *do* know. I don't care about that. What I care about is getting it back. I suspect you're mostly decent, Tony. But I'm not here to appeal to your decency. I'm here to make a deal with you."

"What's the deal?"

"Ten million dollars," Gomez said.

"For what?"

"For letting us know the instant Mason shows up again," Friedkin said. "Because I have a feeling he *will* show up again. And when he does, he's going to come to you."

"Because I'm his friend."

"We already established he has no friends. He has transactional relationships. If you think he's your friend, that's nice, and it's to his advantage. But he's using you, Tony. I think if you go far enough down, you know that. And when you admit it to yourself, letting us know when he resurfaces isn't going to be a problem."

"So all I have to do is let you know he's back, and you drop a bunch of money on me."

"Well, no," Gomez said. "We need to meet with him, and we need to secure the wallet."

"'Meet with him,'" I repeated. "Why do I think that's a euphemism?"

"Mr. Valdez, we know who you are. We know you almost got a job with Chicago PD before the pandemic brought you back to the hospital. Despite that, we know you still work with that detective. We have no illusions you won't speak to her about what we said here. We would not, and will not, ask you to do anything illegal, nor make you an unwitting participant in illegal activity. All we want you to do is help us find Mason. We will take care of everything else, all nice and legal."

"And how will you do that?"

Gomez smiled. "Subpoenas, to start."

"Will you help us, Tony?" Friedkin asked.

"I'll consider it," I said.

"Fair." She nodded to Gomez. "And this is to help you consider."

Gomez handed me what looked like a USB stick.

"Oh, great," I said. "One of these again."

"It's not what you think," Gomez said. "It has access information to an escrow account with ten million dollars in it. Actual dollars, not crypto. You can see it and confirm it exists in reality. When we've talked to Mr. Schilling and gotten back the crypto wallet in his possession, the escrow account will unlock, and then you won't have to work anymore."

"You can be one of the indolent rich, Tony," Friedkin said.

"If you get Mason and the crypto wallet," I said.

"We'd settle for the wallet, to be honest. If you have access to it."

"I told you I don't have it."

"I know. But I thought I'd check again." Friedkin looked over to Gomez. "You can bring in the next two," she said. Gomez nodded and got up.

I took that as my cue and started to get up as well. Friedkin waved me back down. "Stay for longer, Tony."

"I don't want to intrude on your next meeting," I said.

"It will only take a minute," she assured me.

The two men came up to the table with Gomez, who then stepped aside. One of the men looked calm. The other looked like he'd never once in his life stopped sweating. Friedkin did not invite either of them to sit. "Don. Mike," she said. "Thank you for coming to see me."

Don, the calm one, looked over at me. "Who is this?"

"This is Tony Valdez. He's my guest. He's also a dispatcher. Works over at Northwestern Memorial most of the time. In the Critical Care Unit."

"I have a cousin who went in there," Mike, the intensely sweaty man, said to me. "During the pandemic. He didn't come out."

"I'm sorry to hear that," I said.

"Don, Mike, both of you have bids in to be the subcontractor for the electrical systems in the third tower of Fairwood Glen," Friedkin said. She reached over to the table and picked up her expensive bag. "It's taken longer to get back on track than it should've, but we're going to be starting construction within the month. I'm happy to say the final decision on the electrical systems has come down to your two companies. I'm less happy to say your bids are so close in terms of price and substance that they're effectively indistinguishable. The board couldn't decide which of you to award the contract to. I told them I'd let you discuss it between yourselves, and they agreed." She motioned to me. "Tony here will decide who's made the best argument."

With that, Friedkin unlatched her bag, reached in, and used a monogrammed handkerchief to pull out a revolver and set it on the table. She put the handkerchief back into the bag, and set her bag back on the table. She lifted her wine glass.

"Please, discuss," she said.

Don and Mike looked at the revolver, and then looked at me, and then looked at the revolver again.

Don looked over to Friedkin. "You have got to be joking," he said.

Mike, sweating, lunged for the revolver, brought it up point-blank into Don's face, and pulled the trigger.

The revolver clicked. The chamber was empty. Mike looked at the revolver, horrified.

"You *motherfucker*," Don hissed.

Mike went a bright, mottled red, made a small groaning sound, and collapsed on the terrace.

"Interesting," Friedkin said. She took a sip of her wine.

I got up and went to Mike, who was gasping like a fish. "He's having a heart attack," I said after I checked him.

"Is this your professional opinion?" Friedkin asked me.

"I'm not a doctor," I said.

"But you *are* a dispatcher. You have to have *some* diagnostic experience. In your opinion, is this man likely to die without your help?"

"I don't know," I said. I looked at Mike again. He had slipped out of consciousness and wasn't breathing.

Paramedics could be on the scene in minutes, but it was questionable whether he had those minutes to spare. "Maybe. Yes."

"Yes," Friedkin repeated. "All right." She looked at Don. "Congratulations. You get the contract."

Don stared at Friedkin like she was a bug for an entire second. Then he nodded. "Thank you," he said.

Friedkin nodded, finished her wine, grabbed her bag and her book, and stood. "Don. Tony. Thank you for your time." She started to go.

"What about Mike?" I asked, still kneeling by the fallen man.

Friedkin looked at the prone, sweaty Mike. "I'll have Ricardo call 911, if you like."

"He'll be dead before then. I need to dispatch him."

"That's not why I brought you here and I'm not paying for that," Friedkin said.

I stared up at her uncomprehendingly. "What?"

"Tony," she said. "If you want to save him, be my guest. But it's on your own recognizance. And when you talk to your detective friend, you can say whatever you like about what happened here. Just know that I, Ricardo, and Don will all confirm that Mike pulled the gun when I told him Don was awarded the contract, and then he had the heart attack." She motioned to Mike dismissively. "He'll say the same thing if you save him. He has other contracts with us."

"I thought you didn't stab the help," I said.

Friedkin laughed. "Mike's not the help! He's a contractor. And this is how business gets done." She walked off. Don looked at Mike briefly, then followed.

That left Gomez and me, and Mike.

"What are you going to do?" Gomez asked me.

"I need to dispatch him," I said.

"I thought he needed to agree to that."

"He's unconscious," I said. "There's implied consent."

"How are you going to dispatch him?"

I looked at the fallen revolver by Mike's hand, and then glanced up at Gomez. "I don't suppose there are any bullets for that."

Gomez motioned to Mike. "It's *his* weapon," he said. "Maybe you should ask him." He walked away, too, following his boss.

I sat there for a moment with the unconscious, unbreathing man collapsed on the terrace next to me. Then I got up, grabbed his feet, and started dragging him over to the terrace pool.

"And she dared you to tell me about all this," Langdon said to me on the phone. I had been returned to my home with my new USB stick and a number to call if and when I located Mason.

"It wasn't really a dare," I said. "It was more of an announcement that it didn't matter if I did or not. Her version of the story would be the official one."

"And what about the guy you dispatched?"

"Oh, *him*. He called his cell less than a minute after I dispatched him, I would guess from his house phone. Yelled at me for drowning him in the pool. Demanded his clothing and effects back. Told me if I ever talked about dispatching him to anyone, he would personally find me and kick my ass. I reminded him what happened to him the last time he tried to hurt someone."

Langdon chuckled. "Sounds like you made a friend."

"The upshot is it's unlikely he'll support my version of events. Just as Gabrielle Friedkin suggested."

"The next time, record everything, Tony."

"That's not how I usually work," I said.

"Maybe it's time to change how you work."

"I'll keep it in mind. In the meantime, I'm calling the hospital and taking a personal day tomorrow."

"Dispatching someone by drowning them was that traumatic?" Langdon asked.

"It's not that," I said. "I mean, yes, it was. But I want to know a little more about the Friedkins. And I think I know the person to ask."

TWELVE

If you take the Metra train far enough west, it stops being in Chicago and starts being in Oak Park, a small village famed for its Frank Lloyd Wright houses, earthy crunchiness, and voter turnout. I was interested in none of these as I exited the Oak Park Metra station. Rather, I was looking for Home Avenue and a particular house on it.

A few minutes later, I was standing in front of a blue Shaker-style house with red awnings. The house had two signs on the lawn. The first announced that the house was being watched over by a popular home security service. The second announced that the house was for sale.

I went to the door and knocked on it. A minute later the door opened and a hassled-looking bearded man presented himself in the doorway. "You Tony Valdez?" he asked me.

"I am," I confirmed. "And I assume you are Gary Dorn."

"I used to be, anyway," Dorn said. "Now I don't know who the hell I am anymore. I'd shake your hand, but we got over that in the pandemic, didn't we?"

"I guess we did at that."

"I don't miss it. I've had enough clammy, fake handshakes to last me the rest of my life. Not that yours would be clammy."

"It might be," I said. "Now you'll never know."

Dorn gave a short laugh and then looked back briefly into his house. "Do you mind if I don't invite you in? I'm in the process of moving out. It's all boxes and despair in there. A walk might be nice. I could use some fresh air anyway."

"That's fine," I said. Dorn grunted and closed the door on me. He reappeared a minute later, wearing a Cubs hat and an unzipped hoodie. He motioned me south and we started walking down Home Avenue.

"So you're a dispatcher," he said.

"That's right."

"That's a hell of a job, isn't it? Killing people because an actuarial table says it'll save an insurance company x amount of dollars. How long have you been doing it?"

"More than a decade now," I said.

"That's a lot of death."

"Not any more than a doctor or nurse would see. It's mostly not that dramatic."

"No, not as long as you stick with the hospitals," Dorn said. "But I know about the side jobs some of you take."

"Do you."

He nodded. "I was in the early stages of sketching out a story on freelance dispatchers when…" He paused.

"You were laid off from the *Tribune*," I prompted.

"Not laid off," he said. "I took the voluntary buyout. Of course I took the voluntary buyout, because if I didn't they would've laid me off. So six of one and half a dozen of the other. I thought it'd be fine. I had a book coming out, and then I'd do one of those Substacks or Patreons or a podcast or whatever, and I'd keep doing my thing. Then the pandemic hit and the book flopped and my wife told me she wanted a divorce—and my mother got cancer. So I'm selling the house and going back home to fucking Racine, Wisconsin, to take care of Mom while she recovers. *If* she recovers."

"I'm sorry about that," I said.

"Well, thank you. It's kind of you to be sympathetic to my sudden oversharing to a complete stranger. It just kind of sucks to be fifty-eight, suddenly single, and going back to live in your childhood bedroom. I don't recommend it if you can avoid it. You married?"

"I was a long time ago. Not anymore."

"Does being divorced get any easier?"

"It did for me," I said. "But I had work to keep me busy."

Dorn winced. "Ouch."

"Sorry."

He waved it off. "I'll figure myself out. Anyway, this is not why you're here to talk to me. You said you wanted to talk about the Friedkins."

"That's right."

"Because of the book. You read it?"

"I haven't," I admitted. "But last night I visited someone who *was* reading it. Gabrielle Friedkin."

Dorn barked out a laugh. "Okay, you've officially surprised me. I wouldn't have thought she'd bother with it. I know her lawyers did. Or the *family's* lawyers did, in any event. Before it was published, they were threatening me with defamation."

"Is there anything defamatory in the book?"

"Not *really*," Dorn said. "To put that answer in context, I didn't skimp on dishing the dirt on the dead Friedkins, especially Gabrielle's grandfather and great-grandfather, both of whom were real pieces of work. Hell, Woody Guthrie wrote a song about her grandfather. Not a nice one, either. Then again, Guthrie wrote mean songs about a lot of robber barons. All the stuff in there is researched and footnoted and annotated, and even if it wasn't, by law you can't libel the dead."

"What about the living?"

"Them you *can* libel, and there I had to be more careful. The Friedkin family is a holder of a nontrivial number of shares in the conglomerate that owns my publisher, so there was that going on as well. I ended up having to be very circumspect, and corporate legal still demanded I take things out. Gabrielle was reading it, you said?"

"She was in the middle of it when I had my meeting with her."

"What did she say about it?"

"She said it was boring. Sorry."

Dorn nodded. "Well, it's her family's damn fault. If I'd been allowed to keep in the juicy bits about her and her cousins, it would've sold a lot better. Maybe I'd be keeping the house. Why were you meeting with her? Are you friends? Sorry, I probably should've asked that earlier. My personal life collapsing around me has dulled my investigative reflexes."

"We're not friends," I said. "She wanted me to help her find someone."

This got a glance from Dorn. "You moonlight as a private investigator?"

"Not really. It's a mutual acquaintance. He's gone missing. She thinks he might get in touch with me when he resurfaces."

"Will he?"

"It's honestly up in the air at this point."

"What did she offer you to track down your pal?"

"A ridiculous amount of money."

Dorn nodded again. "Of course. Money means nothing to her. Did she hit you with her 'money is transparent' line?"

"As a matter of fact, she did."

"She loves that line. She heard it at a TED Talk once. It's easy to talk about transparent money when you never once had to worry about it. My money is opaque as hell at the moment, I have to say. Who is your friend? Another dispatcher?"

"Yes."

"She loves her dispatchers."

"Tell me what that means," I said.

"Just that she finds ways to have them around."

"I learned that at our meeting," I admitted.

Dorn looked at me sharply. "Feel like telling me about it?"

"I thought you weren't an investigative reporter anymore."

"I'm not, but I like feeling vindicated."

"Tell me what that means."

"It means I had a bunch of stories I absolutely could *not* use, several involving dispatchers, and I'm curious if your story might match up."

"These stories were rumors?"

Dorn snorted. "Hell, no, they are absolutely true, and also absolutely unprovable. The last part is why I couldn't get them published. Truth is an affirmative defense against libel. But if you can't get anyone to say it happened, it makes the stories harder to get past the legal department."

I nodded. "Tell me one of the stories, and I'll tell you what I think about it."

"All right. So, you know the Friedkins made their billions in real estate. Still at it, in fact; they've got several projects up and running around Chicagoland. Their big one in Chicago is that Old Town complex, Fairwood Glen. You know it?"

"I was there last night."

"Sure, at that penthouse, probably. Nice looking. Don't buy it. The roof pool leaks."

"I'll keep that in mind."

"So, real estate," Dorn continued. "But they have their hand in other areas, like billionaires would. The last decade or so, Gabrielle and her generation of cousins got the family involved in tech. Gabrielle started up that venture capital fund. Made a big splash when it was announced. Said the goal was to make Chicago the second Silicon Valley, as if anyone but a real-estate billionaire family would want that."

"Chicago wouldn't want tech jobs?" I asked.

"Tech jobs are fine in themselves. The gentrification that comes with thousands of them being dumped into city neighborhoods without much planning is not so great. Rents go up for everyone, local businesses are priced out, and Chicago stops being Chicago. Great if you own the buildings, not so much if you don't. It's not a coincidence that Gabrielle's venture capital fund popped into existence at the same time the family started a new round of residential tower construction. The plan is to fill them up with tech nerds high on stock options and smugness. Stuff a microbrewery in the basement. Make them think they're having a real urban experience."

"You don't sound happy about it."

"Well, I live in Oak Park, which has a smugness and microbrewery problem of its own, so I'm not casting stones. The point is, even when the Friedkins diversify, they keep an eye on their bread and butter."

"All right."

"They also bring their own distinctive business style to these other fields," Dorn said. "Not union-busting and tenant-crushing, but pitting the people they work with against each other and making them fight for the scraps they toss out. That's a hallowed family tradition. Gabrielle, in particular, indulges. She likes to take the heads of the tech companies she's thinking of investing in, bring them up to that penthouse terrace, and tell them she's only going to invest in one of them and they have to fight to the death for it. That's where the dispatcher comes in, by the way."

"I guessed that," I said.

"And the hell of it is, they do. Fight to the death, I mean. Think about that. Two or three wannabe Zuckerbergs, complete with hoodies, trying to slap fight each other to death. It's a funny image. Horrifying, but funny. My source says Gabrielle sometimes brings an empty handgun and sets it on a table, because she likes the reaction when someone tries to fire it." Dorn looked at me significantly when he said this.

I kept my face blank. "You're not painting a very nice picture of the Friedkins," I said.

"That's because they're not nice and never were," Dorn said. "As I mention several times in my book, which you haven't read. But don't worry about the Friedkins. If they know anything, it's if you splash enough out in philanthropy, you can be as awful as you want. The Friedkins have their name on a lot of academic buildings and art wings. So Gabrielle gets to keep the family tradition of awfulness going for another generation. I mean, it's not just her. All billionaires are terrible almost by definition. Her friend Michel Cadieux, do you know him?"

"I know of him."

"He's a minority partner in that VC fund she has going. Likes to pretend he's clean as a whistle, but the family made its billions doing really shitty things in Indochina back in the day, and isn't much better today. They're in bed with all sorts of appalling people in that area. He's the fresh face on a rotten family. Maybe that's why Gabrielle likes him. They have that in common."

"Why do you think Gabrielle Friedkin does these awful things?" I asked.

"You mean, aside from garden-variety sadism? Dominance. To remind these would-be aspiring tech masters of the universe there's a force greater than them, and before they get to be billionaires on their own, they have to kneel at the altar of the old gods. And to remind them money doesn't come for free, and there's a certain level of capriciousness to who gets it and who doesn't. But mostly, garden-variety sadism."

I chuckled.

"The rich don't usually get where they are by being overly concerned about lives," Dorn said. "But that's mostly lives in an abstract sense. When it comes to individual lives, the ones right in front of them, in my experience the rich are no more bloodthirsty than anyone else. Or at least, they don't want to get their own hands dirty. But if a dispatcher is around, that gives implicit permission for a certain range of activities, let's say. You know about Chekhov's gun, right?"

"Sure," I said. "If you put a gun on the mantelpiece in act one, it's going to get fired in act three."

"That's right. Gabrielle Friedkin plants a lot of Chekhov's dispatchers. Come on, let's cross the street and walk back toward the house."

We crossed and walked back up the street in silence for a bit. "You're worried about your friend," Dorn eventually said.

"I am," I replied.

"You should be," Dorn said. "Not just because he's your friend. Because he represents a weak point in Gabrielle Friedkin's armor. Business associates clam up to keep the money coming. The tech nerds hoping to get funding keep quiet because they need angel investors, or devil investors, in this case. The Friedkins pay and treat their staff well, not because they're good people—they're terrible people, just about all of them—but because they understand that unhappy staff leak. Friedkin staff don't leak. To anyone. Trust me, I spent years trying."

"But dispatchers aren't staff."

Dorn jabbed a finger at me. "Exactly. And while I understand discretion's part of your business model, especially when you take on shady freelance work, at the end of the day your loyalty is to yourself, not your clients. You're a wild card. You said Gabrielle offered you a ridiculous amount of money?"

"She did. She also said she knew I'd talk to my friend at the police about it, and that nothing she's asking me to do would be illegal. Her lawyer said that, I should say."

"That Gomez character."

"That's the one."

"He and Gabrielle met at Northwestern undergrad. He's been her lapdog ever since. He knew a meal ticket when he saw it."

"You don't approve."

"Shit, Valdez, I'm *envious*. I'm selling my house and moving to Wisconsin. I would love to have a meal ticket right about now. I mean, hell. If you don't take Friedkin's deal to sell out your friend, tell her I'd do it for ten percent of what she's paying you."

I smiled.

"But you should know Gabrielle's playing you. Whatever she's offering you, your pal is worth a hundred times that to her. And if she's not concerned about you telling your friends at CPD, it's because she's absolutely certain whatever plan she has for your pal isn't going to come back to her. Something *will* happen to your pal. You know better than anyone how hard it is to keep someone dead these days, but you also know you can do it if you work at it. Do you want my advice?"

"Please."

"One, don't sell out your pal. Friends are hard enough to come by, as it is. My wife got all our friends in the divorce. It sucks. And if I had a million dollars, it would still suck not having friends. Two, find out why she wants your pal, or it's going to end badly for him. Three, take the money if you can."

"You just said I shouldn't sell out my friend."

"That doesn't mean you shouldn't take the money. Look, she's playing you anyway. If I were you, I'd play her back. Especially since, if she used you in your dispatching capacity—which you haven't admitted to but it's obvious to me now that she did—you're in just as much deep shit as your friend. Might as well get paid."

"I'll keep that in mind," I said.

"Please do. And when you do, let me know if you want a house in Oak Park."

My phone rang. It was Langdon. "Where are you?" she asked.

"Oak Park."

"What are you doing in Oak Park?"

"Looking at a house and getting some exercise. I told you I was taking the day off. What are you doing?"

"Looking for you. We've had a development with Paul Cooper."

"Did you find him?" I asked.

"Some of him, yes," Langdon said.

THIRTEEN

"Why is he here?" Andy Liu asked as Langdon and I entered the examining room. Paul Cooper's body— some of it, anyway—lay on the table between us. The medical examiner staff person who led us into the room took this as her cue to leave. It was very quickly the three of us, and some of Cooper.

"Do you have a problem with Tony being here?" Langdon asked.

"I just wasn't aware it was Take Your Informants to Work Day."

"Cute." Langdon motioned to me. "Tony's worked extensively with me and with the Chicago Police Department as a consultant. He was supposed to join the force until the current pandemic changed everyone's plans. Also, he has information material to our mutual investigations."

Liu looked over to me. "And what's that?"

"Gabrielle Friedkin offered me a reward for finding Mason Schilling and that crypto wallet of his."

"Did she. What's the going price?"

"Ten million dollars."

Liu gave a low whistle. "That's not chicken feed. And did you rat out your friend and his wallet?"

"I don't have the wallet and I don't know where Mason is," I said.

"I know you keep saying that. I'm less than one hundred percent convinced." He motioned to Langdon. "The detective here tells me you identified one of the men who stole Cooper's body as Schilling."

"That's right."

"If you pointed us in his direction, it would save us all a lot of trouble. There might even be a reward in it. Not ten million dollars, of course. This is the U.S. government we're talking about. We can't compete with private enterprise."

"I'll keep it mind," I said.

"Do that. Anything else interesting about your meeting with Friedkin?"

"She made two of her contractors fight to the death while I was there."

Liu nodded. "She does that."

"You know about that?" Langdon said, disbelieving.

"Gabrielle Friedkin's been doing the gladiator thing for a while."

"And this doesn't alarm you."

"It's not about being alarmed, it's about what we want to get her for," Liu said. "Be assured, Detective Langdon, when we reel her in, felony attempted murder will be one of the charges we throw at her, if we can get anyone she's made fight for a contract or venture funding to go along with us, which so far we haven't. But there are other more compelling charges we're interested in."

"Like what?" Langdon asked.

"Money laundering, for one. Tax evasion, for another. Fraud for a third." Liu motioned to Cooper's corpse. "This one was helping us build the case against her and a bunch of her pals."

"How was he doing that?" I asked.

"MoreCoinz is a honeypot," Liu said.

I blinked. "You're using the app Cooper made to entrap criminals."

"'Entrap' isn't a word I'm comfortable with," Liu said. "We're not making them use the app. They're using it of their own free will."

"Walk us through this," Langdon said.

"I told you how Cooper'd been working for us. When cryptocurrency took off, we knew it was going to be seen as a vehicle for the rich and the criminal to move their assets in a way they thought we couldn't track. So we had Paul build us a trading platform we could access. And along the way, it became one of the most-used crypto apps in the world."

Langdon looked skeptical. "And no one figured this out."

"Detective, we did the same thing for an 'encrypted' chat app that thousands of criminals used to plan all sorts of felonious activities, and it worked like a charm. We announced a bunch of arrests from it a couple of months ago. Hardly anyone outside of a few nerds knows how encryption works, or what a blockchain is meant to do, how public it is, or whether something is genuinely secure or not. At the end of the day, the vast majority of people think something's secure because someone who they think is knowledgeable tells them it is."

Liu gave a nod here to Cooper's corpse. "Paul had a good reputation among the crypto fans, and we set it up to give MoreCoinz a couple of public victories against governmental intrusion. It made the app look like a safe place to do your dirty business away from the FBI and the IRS. That's all a lot of them needed to be convinced. Not anyone who has a serious understanding of cryptocurrency, of course. None of those people would be moving or trading any of it through an app you download from Apple or Google. But there aren't *that* many of those people."

"So you have the goods on Friedkin," I said.

"Paul did," Liu said. "He knew the app would be cracked and people would be looking for holes in the security, so he designed the app without any back doors. *He* was the back door. Every month or so, he'd do a drop."

"Let me guess," I said. "On a secure crypto wallet."

"That's a good guess. A secure hardware crypt that could be unlocked with his fingerprint, and then required a second encryption key for the data inside to be accessed. The fingerprint part of that is what makes *this* so interesting." Once again, Cooper's corpse got a nod.

A corpse that was missing both of its hands.

"No one saw Cooper's corpse get dropped off?" I asked Langdon, as she drove me back to my apartment.

"He got dumped overnight in an alley in a residential area near Midway Airport," she said. "No security cameras. We're looking through nearby traffic cameras, but we don't know what to look for. Your friend needed a specialized vehicle to steal the corpse. He could've driven a Honda Fit to drop it off."

"That's not great."

"It could've been worse. The body was found early this morning by a local, and we had a car there to deal with it before anyone came by with a cell phone camera. We were able to get it out before the press showed up. As far as anyone knows, the body in the alleyway was a

John Doe, not a billionaire stolen from the ME's office. *We* thought he was a John Doe until he showed up at the examiner's and they recognized him as their lost lamb."

"They're still going to have to explain the missing hands," I pointed out.

"Yes, but that's their problem, not mine," Langdon said.

"You just have to find the hands."

"We know who has the hands. Your friend Mason."

"He just took delivery on the body," I said. "Someone else might have the hands."

Langdon glanced over to me. "I want you to think about what you just said, and the fact your best defense of his actions is 'maybe someone else has the hands.'"

"I'm not defending him. I'm just saying maybe he doesn't have the hands."

"You're sure you don't know where he is right now?" Langdon asked me. "I know I ask this a lot. I keep hoping you'll have a different answer."

"Do you think at this point if I knew where he was, I wouldn't tell you?"

"The fact I'm asking you the question should tell you."

"Ouch."

"Tony, I know you have loyalty to your friends. I'm not saying that's not admirable, most of the time."

"Well, thank you."

"I'm just not sure Mason Schilling is actually a friend of yours."

"You think he's using me."

"I *know* he's using you," Langdon said. "And I know he's relying on your feeling of friendship for him to keep his secrets. I wonder why you'd let him."

"I'd keep your secrets," I said.

"I don't have secrets."

"If you had them, I'd keep them."

"If I had secrets and I told you to keep them, I'd want you to think about why I was asking you to," Langdon said. "And whether keeping them was going to hurt you. Or me."

"You think Mason's in danger," I said.

"Tony, your friend jumped out of a moving car, died, and then came back to steal body parts from a billionaire who was an FBI informant. What about that strikes you as not being the actions of a desperate man?"

"You have a point," I admitted.

"I hate this entire thing," Langdon said. "I hate that I feel like you're keeping secrets from me. I hate that I think you're being used. I hate that the FBI's holding back information from us. I hate that I have billionaires running around my city making people kill each other for sport."

"You think the FBI's holding out on us?" I asked, because I felt like I had to pick a topic.

"Cooper died at Friedkin's party. We know now that before he died, he, Friedkin, Cadieux, Brennan Tunney, and Schilling all disappeared from the party at the same time. Five people conveniently depart, one ends up dead, one disappears, one flees the country, and the two left remaining are untouchable. And the one thing that might explain it all is conveniently missing, and we all have to chase it."

"Tunney's not chasing it."

"He *might* be. *I* haven't been able to get in to ask him. Schilling used to do work for him, didn't he?"

"It's been a few years."

Langdon let out a small laugh. "Time doesn't matter to Tunney. If you get into his orbit, you're in it for the duration. You should know *that*, at least." She turned off of North Avenue onto my street.

"Thanks for the lift," I said, as we pulled up to my apartment.

"You're welcome," Langdon said, as I got out. "Tony, any time you want to really start trusting me again, all you have to do is let me know."

"I do trust you," I said. "More than you know." I closed the car door. Langdon smiled and drove away.

I walked up to my apartment, fished out my keys, opened the door, and took my wallet and mask out of my pocket and placed them on my kitchen counter with my keys. Then I sighed, went to my fridge, and got out a beer.

When all that was done, I looked over to the man sitting on my couch.

"First off, how the hell did you get into my safe?" I asked.

Mason Schilling smiled.

FOURTEEN

"You don't want to know how I am or what I've been doing?" Mason asked lightly.

"I *know* what you've been doing," I said. "Body snatching is a new one for you, Mason."

He chuckled. "You saw that. Well, I suppose you might've. You do hang out with that cop of yours. I imagine that little event caused a stir."

"Why did you do that?"

"Snatch a corpse?"

"Yes."

"I traded a service for protection," Mason said. "It was a fair exchange. Anyway, I wasn't in charge of the operation. I was just a warm body lending a hand."

"Bad pun, Mason."

"I don't know what you mean by that."

"You can't tell me you don't know about the current status of Paul Cooper's corpse," I said.

"Actually, I can," Mason replied. "I helped drop it off. I have no idea what's happened to it since. That's not my department."

"What *is* your department?"

"Recently, it's mostly watching Netflix and trying to stave off boredom. Until a couple of hours ago, when my current…benefactor, who shall remain anonymous, asked me to come see you. May I have a beer?"

"You didn't help yourself to one?" I asked.

"That would be impolite."

"As opposed to, say, taking three thousand dollars from my safe."

"That again." Mason pointed to my bedroom, and presumably to the safe in the closet there. "Go check it."

I stared at him for a minute, and then went to go check the safe. Then I came back to the kitchen, got a beer, and walked it over to Mason, who nodded his thanks.

"Thank you for returning the three thousand dollars," I said, sitting down myself. "And for not taking any of the other money in there."

"Of course," he said. "I also returned your sweats. They're on your bed. They've been laundered. And to answer your first question, your safe has a digital lock and it uses a PIN. Most people reuse PIN numbers, because most people are lazy. I've known your ATM pin for years, because you do a really bad job of hiding it when you take out money. I figured it would be the same for your safe. I was correct. Also, you should change your PIN, obviously. Not changing it *after* I took money from your safe is just sloppy."

"Thank you for the tip," I said sarcastically.

"I'm just trying to be helpful," Mason said, and took a sip of his beer.

"That answers one question I had," I said. "I want to see if you can guess what my next question is."

"Would it be 'why is there now an extra twenty-five thousand dollars in my safe'?" Mason asked.

"Yes. Yes, it would be."

"A little bit of it, you can consider interest on your loan," Mason said. "Maybe about a thousand dollars of it. The rest of it, you can consider payment for babysitting something for me."

"Your crypto wallet," I prompted.

Mason tipped his beer bottle at me. "That's right. I'd like it back now, if you please. More accurately, my benefactor would like it, and at this point I'm inclined to give it to him, all things considered. Well, not *give* it to him. I'm getting a little something for it."

"More than twenty-five thousand dollars, I'm guessing."

"You're not wrong."

"How much?"

"Enough that I won't miss that twenty-five thousand I'm giving you."

"What if I told you I don't have it here?" I asked.

Mason's eyes widened. "Jesus, Tony, I *hope* you don't have it here. I think it's pretty clear this place isn't exactly secure."

"What if I told you I gave it to a cop?"

"Well, that'd make getting it back a little more of a challenge," Mason admitted. "But I have faith in you, Tony." He started to take another sip of his beer.

"And what if I told I'd gotten a better offer for it?"

The beer bottle paused before it hit Mason's lips. "How much better?" he asked.

"Ten million dollars."

Mason chuckled at that. "Gabrielle Friedkin, right?"

"Let's just call them my current benefactor, who shall remain anonymous."

"Ten million dollars is not an anonymous amount of money," Mason said. "That would be Gabrielle, all right."

"She says you stole the wallet from Paul Cooper's corpse, and that it was hers to begin with," I said, abandoning the pretense of anonymity.

"Seems complicated," Mason said. "But a good cover story for offering ten million dollars. If I thought you had any chance of collecting that much from her, I might ask to go in halfsies with you. But you don't."

"It's already in escrow," I said.

"No, her weasel of a lawyer told you it's in escrow, and you don't have the means to confirm whether he's actually telling you the truth. Trust me, Tony. I've spent a lot of time with Gabrielle Friedkin and her pals over the last year. They're anglerfish, and money is their bright and shiny lure. It gets you close to them. Then you get the teeth."

"*You* took their money," I pointed out.

"And I had to jump out of a moving car to get away from them." Mason spread his arms wide. "This is my point to you. I'm speaking from experience. The twenty-five thousand you already have from me is worth far more than the ten million you will never, ever get. We're rabble to them. The rich don't feel obliged to treat the rabble fairly. Shit, they stab each other in the eye every chance they get."

"Yet you trust *your* anonymous benefactor."

"I never said I trust him," Mason said. "I offer him a practical and tactical advantage he's willing to pay for. That's as good as it gets in this world."

"When all this started, you told me what you had on that crypto wallet was money."

"It does have money on it."

"No one's going to offer me ten million dollars to get your forty thousand, Mason."

"Yes, you're right. It's not just money. Paul Cooper left me something else on the wallet."

"What?"

"Complete administrative access to MoreCoinz."

I paused. "Excuse me?"

"Right?" Mason said. "That's what I thought."

"He gave administrative access to you."

"Yes."

"Were you friends?"

"The only time I ever met him was at Gabrielle's billionaire scheming parties."

"So why would he do that?"

Mason waved his arms, sloshing the beer in his bottle. "How the fuck do I know? I don't need it. I don't want it. I definitely didn't *ask* for it. I didn't even know I *had* it, until a bunch of goons came into my house and grabbed me and the wallet and stuffed it and me into their goddamn SUV."

"Whose goons?"

"Gabrielle's, almost certainly. All of this shit is organized and run by her. She and Paul were using MoreCoinz to hide money and bilk a bunch of tech dickheads who thought they were buying in to her venture capital fund. That fund was why she kept me around."

"For the gladiator thing."

Mason looked at me funny. "The what?"

"The gladiator thing. Someone called it that to me recently. She'd make the guys angling for her venture capital battle for it."

"I wouldn't call watching a bunch of untoned tech nerds trying to choke each other a 'gladiator thing.' Maybe 'Flabby Fight Club.'"

"You were there when Paul Cooper died," I said.

"I wasn't in the room, no," Mason said. "My services weren't being called for yet."

"What do you mean?"

"Gabrielle and her brain trust were having a pregame meeting. I was there and Cooper paid me in advance. He handled the funds. I was going to be brought in when they started 'interviewing' the tech dweebs they were thinking of funding."

"So the party wasn't just a party."

"I'm sure it was just a party for some of the people who were there. But not for Gabrielle and Cooper and the others."

"So you didn't see what happened to Paul Cooper."

Mason shook his head. "I saw Gabrielle, her weasel lawyer, and the others go into the study she uses as her office. When they did that, I went to take a dump. As I was finishing up there was a loud bang."

"Nobody panicked?"

Mason shrugged. "It could've been a gunshot. It could've been the caterers opening a champagne bottle. About a minute after the bang, I saw Gomez open the door of the study, look around for me, and wave me in. I went in and Cooper was on the floor, already dead.

I confirmed he was gone and there was nothing I could do for him. By this time, someone else at the party had figured out what happened and called 911. Gabrielle's flunky lawyer told me to go home, and if anyone asked, to say I was at the party as a guest, not there professionally. He also told me to hold off transferring my fee from MoreCoinz for a couple of days, to support that 'at the party as a guest' thing until Paul's death was ruled a suicide and the police lost interest."

I got what he was saying. "You didn't know he sent you anything other than access to your tip."

"I found out because one of the goons who stuffed me into the Escalade was talking about it on his phone. He was holding the wallet in one hand and his phone in the other. I grabbed the wallet, opened the door, and fell out onto the Dan Ryan."

"And got hit by a Tesla."

"Which I survived," Mason pointed out.

"Technically you *didn't*," I reminded him. "And when I got to you in the hospital, you were ready to die."

"I wasn't ready to die. I just preferred dying relatively quickly to the long and painful death I'd suffer if I came back and got nabbed again. And I would've gotten nabbed again. Except for you."

"I'm your friend, Mason."

"I'm glad you think so."

"Don't you?"

"Since we're friends, you won't have any problem getting that wallet back to me," Mason replied, avoiding answering the question I had put to him.

"It will take some doing," I said.

"That almost sounds like a euphemism for 'I'm not going to get that wallet back to you,'" Mason said.

"It's not a euphemism," I said. "I have the wallet somewhere safe. Getting it back will take a bit of doing. As in, I'm not going to be able to get it to you today."

"When *can* you get it to me?"

"Is there a rush?"

"Now that you mention it, yes, there is."

"I'm going to need to get back to you on that," I said.

Mason pointed toward the bedroom. "Twenty-five thousand dollars," he said. "Paid in advance."

"You asked if there was going to be a problem getting that crypto wallet back to you," I reminded him. "This is me telling you there won't be. If you don't rush me."

"I trusted you with that thing," Mason said.

"Then trust me to get it back to you. And trust me when I say it will take some doing."

Mason looked at me, unhappy. "I need it in the next couple of days, Tony," he said. "Otherwise, things get... uncomfortable for me."

"Lead with that information next time," I suggested.

"I would like for there to be a next time," Mason said. "That's why I'm here." Then he slugged back the rest of his beer and put the bottle on the floor. "Speaking of which, I need to make myself scarce again."

"How can I get in touch with you?" I asked.

"You can't." He stood. "I'll come around again."

"Knock the next time," I suggested.

"Change your PIN," Mason said. He left out the door.

I pulled out my phone and called Nona Langdon.

"I was just about to call you," she said as she picked up. "We've had a development."

"You tell me yours and I'll tell you mine," I said. I walked to the front of the condo, to the windows that overlooked the street. Mason would be coming out of the front of the building any second now.

"Cody Williamson's gone missing."

"Since when?"

"Since sometime this morning. He didn't show up to his meeting with his lawyer. His lawyer went to his apartment and got the building manager to let him in. Williamson's not there. Phone, wallet, and ID are there, though."

"That's not good," I said. Mason had stepped out of the building now and was walking toward the street.

"We talked to the neighbors. No one saw anything. There are security cameras on the building, but the ones for the fire escape had their SD cards snatched."

"That's not suspicious at all."

"The building manager says neighborhood kids steal them all the time, so maybe it's not. What's your development?"

A black Cadillac Escalade drove up alongside Mason, passenger-side window down. A man leaned out of the window and aimed something at him. Two small projectiles fired and hit him. Mason stiffened and fell. He'd been tased.

"Oh, shit," I said. I dropped the phone and ran out of my apartment and down the stairs.

I got outside just after Mason had been bundled into the Escalade. The vehicle was taking off down the street. I tried to read the license plate, and reached for my phone to take a photo of it as it drove off. Then I remembered I'd dropped the phone, with Langdon still on it.

"Shit," I said again. I turned in time to see someone walking toward me, holding out a Taser. Several thousand volts of electricity blew out my consciousness and I slid into darkness.

FIFTEEN

I came to in blackness, which, after a moment, I realized was not because I was trapped in darkness, or blind, but because I had a bag over my head. I tried to move, but a hand pushed on me.

"Sit still and be quiet, or I'll zap your ass again," a voice said.

I sat still and paid attention to my surroundings. There was road noise and vibration. I was in a car. This suggested I had not been out for that long. I had questions, but I also didn't want to get electrified again. I decided to wait.

An indeterminate amount of time later, the car came to a stop and I heard the sound of a garage door opening. The car moved forward and the garage door closed. I was hustled out of the car and led through a door and down some stairs. I was put onto a couch, and my hands and feet zip-tied. The bag came off.

I was in a nondescript finished basement. On one side of me, zip-tied, was Mason. On the other side of me, also zip-tied, was Cody Williamson. Both of them had duct tape over their mouths.

In front of me, sitting comfortably on a simple wooden chair, was Michel Cadieux.

"I have questions," I said, after a moment.

Cadieux spread his hands. "By all means."

"How are you here?" I began.

"I never left," Cadieux said. He pointed to Williamson. "I heard my idiot subordinates get arrested at your apartment and assumed I'd soon be getting a visit from the Chicago Police. For various reasons, I've long had a plan for making it look like I'd suddenly left the country without benefit of a plane or passport. I put it into effect. We had to wait for you and the detective to show up in the building, so you could hear the gunshot and infer from there. Everything else was simple."

"I saw you in your house in Lyon."

"You saw me in front of an 8K screen in our virtual conference studio one floor down. When you were coming up in the elevator, I took the stairs. I use the Lyon home shot when I'm teleconferencing with European partners. They like it when I pretend I'm on the same continent. Business psychology. You and your detective fell for it, too, which was useful. You didn't go looking for me. Neither did the police."

I looked around the basement. "And you've been here since then?"

"Not in this basement, no."

"Where are we?" I asked.

"We're somewhere in the Chicagoland area."

"And you're not worried about anyone coming to search your basement?"

"It's not *my* basement. It's an Airbnb, rented through an intermediary, not traceable to me or my company. We've got a week rental. We're not going to be disturbed anytime soon."

I glanced over to Williamson. "Why is he here?"

"I just recently learned he's an FBI informant. That was...disappointing. I can't have him running around. He's not important to why you're here, Tony. He just happens to be here."

I motioned my head to Mason. "And him?"

Cadieux smiled. "He's very connected to why you're here. As I'm sure you know."

"Explain it to me."

"I want Mason's crypto wallet. I took it from him once, and he managed to get it back. He doesn't appear to have it anymore. I suspect he gave it to you. I'd like you to give it to me. And I'd appreciate it, Tony, if you didn't pretend you don't know what I'm talking about."

He nodded at Williamson. "After all, you tried to entrap this one with a fake version."

"You were the one who kidnapped Mason before," I said. "The one he jumped out of an SUV to get away from."

"Some of my people, yes," Cadieux said, and grimaced slightly. "That was embarrassing. I didn't think he'd jump out of a car on a freeway. I learned a lesson."

I let out a small, short chuckle.

"What's funny?" Cadieux asked.

"I thought it was Gabrielle Friedkin who snatched him," I said.

"I'm sure the thought occurred to her. I happened to get to him first."

"So you want me to give you his crypto wallet," I said.

"I do," Cadieux said. "And something else."

I frowned. "What else is there?"

"You and your detective fell for the gunshot, but you did something I didn't expect. You went through my trash."

I nodded. "I found a crypto wallet of yours."

"I put it in the trash to clear off the desk and keep your detective from noticing it. I wasn't expecting custodial to come through when they did. And I didn't expect *you* would root through the garbage. Can you tell me why you did that?"

"Call it a hunch."

"I need it back, too," Cadieux said.

"There's a problem there," I said. "The Chicago Police have it."

"That *is* a problem," Cadieux agreed. "But it's your problem."

"They're not going to give it to me. They're busy trying to break into it."

Cadieux waved dismissively. "They're as likely to break into it as you are to turn into a unicorn. That's not why I need it."

"Why *do* you need it?"

"As far as you're concerned, Tony, I need it because I need it. I need it, and I need Mason's wallet."

"You're not the only one who wants it," I said.

Cadieux smiled. "You've had other offers for it. Gabrielle, I assume. Maybe one or two others. I imagine you've been promised substantial incentives."

"Maybe," I said.

"Well, fair enough," Cadieux said, and reached inside his jacket to a pocket there. "Allow me to offer my own incentive package to you." He pulled out a multifunction tool and thumbed open the knife. It clicked into place. Cadieux leaned over and drove it into Mason's leg, into the muscle right above his knee.

Mason screamed through the duct tape and thrashed about, knocking the knife out of the wound. Blood began to seep into his jeans.

After Mason composed himself, Cadieux calmly reached down and picked up his multi-tool. He wiped the blade on Mason's jeans, cleaning off the blood. He closed the knife, put it away, and turned his attention back to me.

"You're a dispatcher, like Mason here," Cadieux said. "So I know you know a few things. I know you know that if you kill someone, when they come back, their bodies are like they were a few hours before. So if I were to kill Mason now, by shooting him, or cutting his throat, when he came back, he wouldn't be shot, or his throat cut, or"—he tapped Mason's wound, making Mason give a pained grunt—"even have this little wound here. Yes?"

"That's right," I said.

"Ah! But if I kill Mason tomorrow, then when he comes back, *this* wound"—another tap, another groan—"will be there. Enough time has passed. I looked you up, Tony, after our meeting. I know you work in a hospital, in a critical care unit. I imagine when you talk to families who want you to dispatch their loved ones, you tell them this. There's only so much damage a dispatch will reset. Yes?"

"Yes."

"So here's my incentive package to you, Tony. I'm going to give you a day to get me both of those crypto wallets. After that, every hour on the hour, Mason here loses a body part. We'll start with toes. Then fingers.

Then ears. Then eyes. And if after two whole days, you have nothing for me, I'll have his nose cut off. And then after that"—Cadieux spread his hands—"well, after that, it's just a matter of time, isn't it? How much of Mason you get back depends on how quickly you move. And of course, on whether you choose to dispatch him or not when I return him. I'll leave that detail to you."

I looked over to Mason, who was breathing heavily from his nose. Next to me, Cody Williamson was also breathing heavily. He knew what was going to happen to him wasn't even under discussion at the moment.

"Is this incentive package acceptable to you?" Cadieux asked.

"No," I said.

Cadieux smiled, it seemed, despite himself. "*Really.* Well, Tony, this is a bold move I wasn't expecting. I'm curious to see how it plays out."

"I want Cody in the package."

"He's not part of the deal."

I shook my head. "I'm pretty sure you found out he worked with the FBI because I tried to entrap him," I said. "That means the reason he's here right now is because of me. That makes him part of the deal. I get you those wallets, you give me both of them."

"And if I say no?"

"Then you can go fuck yourself, because I'm not going to help you."

"I love how you think this is a negotiation," Cadieux said, after he was done laughing. "It's not."

"Whatever is on those wallets is important enough that you stayed in this country instead of fleeing to France, where you wouldn't be extradited," I said. "It's important enough that you kidnapped Mason twice. It's important enough that you sent people to break into my house. It's important enough that you're threatening me with the mutilation of my friend."

"I could threaten *you* with mutilation as well," Cadieux noted.

"You could," I agreed. "Which just goes to my point. Whatever it is you get with those wallets, you don't just *want* it. You *need* it. Which means you need me and my cooperation. And my terms are Mason and Cody. Both."

Cadieux stared at me. Then he turned to Cody Williamson. "Well, Cody? Do you want in on this little deal? You should know anything I do to him"—he pointed to Mason—"I'm going to do to you. Right after I'm done with him. Finger for finger. Eye for eye. Your choice."

Williamson looked sidelong at me. He slowly nodded.

"Fine," Cadieux said. "Both of them."

"And thirty-six hours before you start cutting into either of them."

Cadieux shook his head. "No, we won't be changing that. And if you try to argue with me about that, I'll start the cutting clock right now."

I scowled but said nothing. I nodded.

"Good. One other thing. Your detective friend. You can't go to her."

"The cops have your crypto wallet, and you don't want me to go to the one cop who might actually help me?" I asked.

"That's right. She strikes me as more ethical than you, Tony. And of course that would be a problem. So, no, you can't go to her. You can manage that, yes?"

"I suppose I'll have to," I said.

Cadieux clapped his hands and stood up. "Then we have a deal."

"How will I reach you when I have the wallets?" I asked.

"Put the HowlRound messaging app on your phone," Cadieux said. "And do me a favor—put a PIN on your phone. Once you sign in on the app, I'll have someone contact you. You can verify it's who you're meant to talk to because they'll put the word 'digit' at the top of the message."

"All right."

Cadieux smiled. "I'm glad we can do business, Tony. I wish you success, both for yourself, and for these two. Now, be patient, someone will come get you in a moment. I just have to do this first." He reached down, took the bag off the floor, and put it back on my head. "There we go. Good luck, Tony. Be in touch soon." I heard him get up and walk up the basement steps.

"Mason, Cody," I said, through the bag. "I'm going to do the best I can."

I heard nothing from either of them besides breathing.

I heard someone coming down the steps and sensed someone standing over me.

"The bag stays on until we get you home," a voice said, the same one I had heard earlier. "We'll get you out of the zip ties, but if you cause us any trouble, I'll put a zip tie around your neck. Got it?"

"Got it," I said.

There was silence for a moment, then a click, and then someone moved over my hands and feet, severing the zip ties. "Stand up," the voice said.

I stood up.

There was another silence, and I could feel the man moving around me. "You don't have your phone or wallet on you," he said.

"They're at home," I said.

"So, no valuables."

"Not on me."

"Well, shit," the voice said, and I could hear the rustling of fabric. "That makes getting you home a hell of a lot easier."

I realized what he meant by that a fraction of a second before he shot me point-blank in the head.

SIXTEEN

For the second time in my life, I died.

For the record, I didn't like it any better than the first time.

Like the first time, after I was murdered I found myself falling, naked, into my own bed. The bed was in a different apartment than it was the first time; in fact, it was a different bed, because the first bed had burned up in a fire. It was still my bed, in my apartment; the place where I felt I belonged, the place, more than anywhere else in the world, I felt safe. My place of home.

And like the first time, the thing I did immediately after returning was throw up.

Unlike the first time, I managed to roll off the bed and stumble into the bathroom before I threw up. Most of what came up made it into the toilet. As I was doing so, some quiet, calm, and undeniably strange part of my brain wondered about what I was currently regurgitating into the toilet bowl—When had I eaten that? What · was the rationale for whatever it was that made us come back after death to include what was in our digestive system?—but mostly, I was simply and purely spilling my guts.

When I was done, and while I was resting my head on the toilet bowl, eyes closed, I heard someone walk up behind me. I opened my eyes and turned my head slightly to see. Nona Langdon was there, gun trained on me.

"Well, this is awkward," I finally said.

"Jesus, Tony," Langdon said. "What happened?"

"I mean…" I waved awkwardly at my current state.

"Who did this to you?"

"It's complicated."

"I'm *guessing*," Langdon said.

I frowned, my head still on the toilet bowl. "Why are you here?"

"Tony, the last thing I hear from you are the words, 'Oh, shit,' and then I don't hear anything," she said. "What do you *think* I'm doing here?"

"I like that you care," I said. "At the moment, it's really inconvenient. But I still like it."

"What do you mean, it's really inconvenient?"

I waved toward my bedroom. "Could you get me my bathrobe?"

Langdon nodded, holstered her handgun, and disappeared for a second. She reappeared with my robe, a basic gray cotton thing. She tossed it to me and then headed back to the living room.

I dragged the robe to me, got up, and put it on. I swayed for a moment and leaned on the sink. I rinsed out my mouth, and after a moment of considering, brushed my teeth. With Langdon watching me, I went to my kitchen, got a glass and water from the sink. I drank the entire glass and then got another.

"You all right?" she asked.

"I remember you asking me that the first time I died," I said.

"Yeah, you beat up my car interior."

"My answer hasn't changed." I drank some more. "Your being here is inconvenient, because I was told not to go to you."

"Who told you that?"

"The person who has Mason Schilling and Cody Williamson and is threatening to trim them down one finger at a time until I give him what he wants. I was with both of them, and the person holding them."

Langdon narrowed her eyes. "Who is this?"

"Telling you costs fingers. The fact you're here right now would cost them fingers if he knew."

"You didn't come to me. I was already here."

"I don't think that sort of rules lawyering is going to be allowed," I said.

"Then tell me what I can do," Langdon said.

"You can give me your car keys," I said.

"Excuse me?"

"Your car keys. Please."

Langdon looked at me doubtfully, but she fished her keys from her pocket and slid them over to me on the kitchen counter.

I picked them up. "Stay here and stay away from windows," I said, and went out to the street in my robe. If I had any sort of sense, I would've put myself into pants, or at least sweats. But I wasn't exactly working at full capacity.

Langdon's car was down the street a bit. I opened it with the key fob and fished through the glove compartment until I found what I was looking for. I closed the car back up and looked around to see if anyone was watching me. The street was quiet, and no one appeared to be hanging out in their car. I went inside and offered Langdon back her keys.

"Why did you need my keys?" she asked as she took them from me.

"I needed to get this," I said, opening my left hand. In my palm was the crypto wallet that Mason had given me.

Langdon's eyes widened when she saw it. "You asshole," she said. "You had it the whole time."

I shook my head. "*You* had it the whole time. Well, most of the time. Since we did that swap with Williamson at the Bean. I put it in there when I got some tissues."

"You told me before then you didn't have it."

"I told you that when you were holding it and I wasn't."

Langdon shot me a look. "Are you actually serious right now?"

I shrugged and put the crypto wallet into my robe pocket. "Technically correct is the best kind of correct."

"And here you are accusing *me* of rules lawyering. No matter how you rationalize it, you lied to me, Tony."

"I lied to you," I acknowledged. "I'm not going to excuse it. I was doing it because I thought Mason was in danger and I thought keeping the wallet safe would keep him safe. Especially when so many people came for it."

"So, you just tried to excuse lying to me."

"Not an excuse. An explanation."

"That's more rules lawyering, Tony," Langdon said. "You had me chasing around Chicago for something I had in my glove compartment."

"I wanted it safe," I said. "I knew it would be safe with you. And I wanted you safe, too."

"I'm a goddamn cop, Tony!"

"And I promise you the people I'm dealing with right now don't give a single shit about that," I said. "They absolutely would go right through you to get this thing."

Langdon looked at me, and I could tell she was running through several different responses in her mind, and one by one rejecting them. What finally came out was, "You and I are going to have a serious talk about a lot of things very soon."

"I'm sure we are," I said. "Thank you."

"For what?"

"For not saying everything else that's going through your head right now. Or arresting me."

"Don't tempt me."

"I'm going to try very hard not to," I promised.

Langdon pointed to the pocket of my robe. "I don't suppose you want to give that to me now. Actually and officially."

"I can't," I said. "I need it."

"I thought you said you weren't going to tempt me to arrest you. That's evidence."

"It's also the one thing that's keeping all of Mason's fingers in place. And Cody Williamson's, come to think of it."

"At the very least, I need to tell Agent Liu we know where both of them are."

I shook my head. "We don't."

"You just said you were there with them."

"I was tased and transported with a bag over my head. Then I traveled by bullet. I don't know where I was. The only thing I know is, it was in the Chicagoland area. That could be anywhere from Aurora to Waukegan. I know they're alive, and for now, they're in one piece. Other than that, I can't tell you. And if you tell Liu any of this at the moment, you risk Mason's and Williamson's future."

"You want me to lie to Liu."

"You don't have to lie. Just maybe don't take his calls for a little while."

"Then what am I supposed to do?"

"You're supposed to trust me for that same little while."

"Well, there's a problem with that, Tony. You asked me to trust you before, and look where we are now."

"How about this, then. You don't have to trust me, but I'm asking you to give me little bit of time to fix things. And to stay away from me until I do."

"How much time?"

"The clock I'm working under is twenty-four hours."

"What happens then?"

"Those fingers go missing. For a start."

"First hands, now fingers," Langdon said, and then caught the involuntary grimace I made. "What?"

"I asked Mason about Paul Cooper's hands," I said.

"And?"

"He said he didn't know anything about them. Whatever happened was after his involvement with the corpse."

"Considering his current situation, how truthful do you think that is?" Langdon asked.

"As truthful as anything from Mason ever is."

"So, not a lot," Langdon said.

I shrugged again. There wasn't much to say about that.

"Speaking of Cooper, Andy Liu heard from Cooper's parents," Langdon said. "Their lawyers, anyway. The tech people at MoreCoinz have been locked out of the back end of the app. Cooper set it up so that if he doesn't check in every few days, no administrative work can be accessed."

"Why would he do that?" I asked.

"Apparently it was one of his fail-safes against hacking. The app's working fine for now, but the tech people say as soon as there's a major tech issue, the app will halt trading and other functions, including user access to their online digital wallets."

"So when that happens, billions in cryptocurrency will be inaccessible."

"That's the gist of it. The tech people are under the impression that if they get the parents to work together, they can legally get access to Cooper's administrative account and start the reset. Liu tells me this was all news to both sets of lawyers." Langdon looked at me. "Now. Does this have anything to do with what you're doing?"

"I don't know," I said. "That's part of what I have to figure out."

"And how're you going to do that?" she asked.

"I think it might be time to call in a favor," I said.

SEVENTEEN

Early the next morning, a black town car rolled up to my apartment building. The driver got out, opened the passenger door, and invited me in. The door closed behind me, and I was quietly and efficiently transported out of the city to Evanston, directly north of Chicago. The house I was driven to had been constructed at the turn of the previous century. It had gables and round sitting rooms, and a lovely wrap-around porch that was visible as we drove onto the property.

I was not going to the house. I was going to the coach house behind it, a more modest affair that merely looked like a normal Evanston home. It would comfortably fit the family of a podiatrist or Northwestern University classics professor. It must be nice, I thought, to have an upper-middle-class home that functioned as one's garage.

The car stopped and the driver came to open my door. A man was waiting for me as I stepped out.

"Mr. Valdez," he said. "I'm Henry Donnelly, Mr. Tunney's executive assistant. He's waiting for you in his study. Follow me, please."

Brennan Tunney's study was on the second floor of the coach house. It was bright and airy and minimalist, and looked for all the world like the home office of a junior vice president of a social media company. It didn't look like the office of the CEO of a corporation born from the Prohibition-era Irish mob and debatably legitimate in the modern day.

Tunney, behind his desk, seemed to catch the expression in my eyes. "You look disappointed, Tony," he said. He didn't get up to meet me. I didn't expect him to.

"This office wasn't what I was expecting," I said. "Or where."

"You were expecting wood paneling and me stroking a kitten."

"I'm not sure. Maybe. Yes."

"I do have a cat. It's in the house. I could have it fetched."

"That's all right," I assured him.

"As for the rest of it, my wife wanted to live in the suburbs. Better schools. That sort of thing. I'd rather have stayed in Chicago, but it's important to have a calm and happy family life. So here I am in Evanston."

"It's nice," I said.

"Thank you. I do wonder what Dad would've thought of it. He considered himself an old school mobster to the end. Kept quiet about it the last few years out of respect to me, which I appreciated." Tunney motioned at the office. "But he would definitely consider this selling out."

"I heard about your father's passing," I said. Fintin Tunney, the last of the great Chicago Irish mobsters, had died early in the recent pandemic. "I'm sorry for your loss."

"Thank you. My father was old and in poor health as it was."

"You could've had him dispatched. The Family Compassion Act would've allowed for it."

Tunney smiled at me. "I think of all people, Tony, you know that law isn't as compassionate as it was advertised to be, then or now. It was my father's time, and neither I nor anyone else in the family saw the point in delaying what was coming. Besides,"—he motioned to encompass the minimalist office—"my father was the last of the Tunneys with a connection to our previous line of work. His passing helped put a cap on certain aspects of our family business."

"Did it?"

"Publicly, yes. Privately, there are still a few bits to work out."

"I'm not going to lie to you, those bits are why I'm here."

Tunney smiled. "I like that you think I don't know that." He motioned to a chair in front of his desk. "Sit, Tony. Tell me what's on your mind."

I sat. "You once said you owed me a favor."

"I did say that," Tunney agreed. "And do you remember what I said to you about it?"

"You said, 'Choose well. Choose wisely.'"

"It always surprises me how few people actually do that," Tunney said. "Choose wisely. Most people squander the favor I owe them. Usually on money. Occasionally on revenge. So rarely on anything useful."

"I need that favor from you now," I said.

"Of course. What do you need?"

"I need something retrieved out of a Chicago Police evidence room."

Tunney sat quietly for a moment. "Perhaps I didn't make the 'choose wisely' part clear enough," he said.

"You did, I promise."

"You know, Tony, for a long time it was clear you didn't want this favor from me. I understood that, and I understood your wish to stay clear of me and my business as much as you could. And obviously it did me no harm *not* to have you collect on the favor. But now—this."

"I have a good reason for it," I said.

"I would hope so," Tunney replied. "And while I wouldn't put you under the obligation to explain your wish, if you want to tell me I'd be happy to hear it."

"To save the life of my friend."

"That's dramatic," Tunney said. "And also, these days, usually unnecessary."

I looked at Tunney levelly. "You know as well as I do that it can be managed."

"With patience, time, and silence," Tunney said. "I said that to you as well."

"Time is actually a problem here," I said. "I was told I had twenty-four hours. That was as of last night."

"What happens when the clock runs out?"

"Hands start missing fingers. And then things get worse from there."

Tunney nodded. "I see where this is going. The more time you take, the less of your friend there is to retrieve at the end of it."

"Something like that," I said.

"What you're asking is difficult," Tunney said.

"I know that. It's why I need the favor."

"What is it you need to have taken from our friends at the Chicago Police Department?"

"A crypto wallet," I said. "Forgive me for asking, but you know what that is?"

"I live and do business in the twenty-first century, Tony, so yes," Tunney said. "What's so special about this crypto wallet?"

"It belongs to Michel Cadieux," I said.

Brennan looked at me for a moment, and then did something I wasn't expecting.

He laughed.

He laughed loudly and at length. It was unnerving.

The door to the study opened and Henry Donnelly came in, a look of concern on his face. Tunney, still laughing, waved him back out the door. Before he left he shot me a look, as if to say, *What the hell did you do?* I shrugged as he closed the door behind him.

"Well, this puts a new spin on things," Tunney said, when he'd finished laughing. Then he looked at me. "Are you okay, Tony?"

"Yes," I said. "I'm sorry. I don't think I've ever seen you do that before."

"Laugh?"

"Yes, that."

"I'm a human being, Tony."

"No, I understand that," I assured him.

"You should've told me what you wanted when you came in," Tunney said.

"I didn't know it would provoke...*this*." I waved at Tunney.

"But you knew that I'm not, shall we say, a neutral observer of Michel Cadieux's business."

"I know you and he run in the same circles."

"That's one way of putting it," Tunney said. "Cadieux and I have similar backgrounds, when it comes to our family business histories. I think of him as being less financially prudent than I am, which is probably why you're in the position you're in now."

"I don't know what that means," I said.

"It's not important at the moment, although you might look into it when you leave. Now. Your friend who's in imminent danger. I'm going to suppose it's Mason Schilling."

"Yes," I said.

"And you have his crypto wallet?"

"Maybe," I hedged.

Tunney caught that. "If I wanted his wallet, Tony, I would've already had it, and not let Schilling get away on the Dan Ryan Expressway."

"You know about that."

"I do," Tunney said. "And more than that, as well. I know why Cadieux wants that wallet back."

"Why?"

"Because if he doesn't get it back, he can't get his money out of that MoreCoinz app. If he doesn't get his money out of the app before Paul Cooper's fail-safe goes into effect, he's going to be unhappy."

"How do you know about that?" I asked.

"About Cadieux being unhappy?"

"About Paul Cooper's fail-safe."

"I think you know I knew Paul Cooper. You may assume we talked business."

"Just how unhappy is Cadieux going to be?"

"Unhappy enough to dismember Mason Schilling, for a start."

"And Cody Williamson."

"I don't know who that is," Tunney said.

"He worked for Cadieux. Also a snitch for the FBI."

"One of Andy Liu's?" Tunney asked.

I blinked. "You know about the FBI thing?"

Tunney smiled. "Given my family's business history, it's useful to know the players in the city."

"Which is why you knew Cadieux and Gabrielle Friedkin and Paul Cooper in the first place," I suggested.

"In a way, yes," Tunney said. "Although that was more of a business arrangement."

"Knowing what I know of these people, I wouldn't have anything to do with them."

"It's not sensible for someone like you to do business with them," Tunney agreed. "I see some personal advantages, however. Tony, I'll let you in on something. Do you know why I was so determined to get my family out of its previous line of business?"

"You didn't want to go to prison, was my guess."

Tunney chuckled, which was vastly preferable to a long laughing session. "That's true. But not the actual reason. The actual reason, Tony, is that these days it's so much easier to make money legitimately. For decades, my father and his father had to worry about getting tripped up on taxes from their endeavors or getting caught by law enforcement. Now the Tunney businesses pay almost nothing in taxes, and it's due to entirely legal business expenses, deductions, and activities. You have to work at it to pay taxes. It's almost perfect."

"Almost," I said.

"The problem is greed," Tunney said.

"Excuse me?"

"Greed," Tunney repeated. "Not the greed of criminals. The greed of legitimate businesspeople. They're making money in the billions. Hand over fist. More than any one person could spend or any one company could use. It's still not enough." He waved in the direction of Chicago. "That's why Mason Schilling's in the position he's in right now. Michel and Gabrielle got greedy and then got themselves out too far on a financial ledge— not the same ledge, but two ledges right next to each other. Your friend Mason got in the middle of that. Accidentally, yes; he was just there for the scraps they were throwing to him. But he still got caught up in it."

"You were there, too," I reminded Tunney.

"I understand this may make my lecture on greed ring somewhat hollow," Tunney allowed. "But in time— in a very short time, if we're going to help you help Mason Schilling—you'll know why I'm telling you this." He clapped his hands. "In the meantime, Tony, I'm going to grant your favor."

I felt relief wash over me. "Thank you."

"Don't thank me, I owed it to you. And once it's done, I have no further obligation to you. With that said, if you're inclined to be useful, there's something else you can do for me."

"What is it?"

"Is that you agreeing to be useful?" Tunney asked.

"It's me not having made up my mind."

"Fair enough. Go home, Tony. You'll get a package soon. The crypto wallet will be in it. If you just want to trade Mason Schilling for it, then our business will be concluded."

"And if not?"

"Then there'll be other things in the package, too," Tunney said. "I feel confident you'll know what to do with them when you see them."

The package arrived at noon, by way of a perfectly normal courier who, I have to assume, had no idea what she was carrying and from whom. As promised, Michel Cadieux's crypto wallet was there—along with a few other things, and an unsigned note, which read:

> *Everything you need is here. See if you can connect the dots. What you do with them once you do is up to you.*

I spent an hour with the contents of my package, and then I opened my phone and accessed the HowlRound communication app, which I had downloaded earlier. A single message was there, from what I assumed was a burner number, with a single word in it: *digit.*

I have the items, I texted back.

Thirty seconds later, a voice call popped up in the app. I let it through.

"Please hold," a voice said.

A few seconds after that, Michel Cadieux got on the line. "You have them, then."

"I do."

"I'm glad to hear that. I wondered how close you were going to come to the deadline. How did you get them, if you don't mind me asking?"

"I have friends. Aside from Detective Langdon."

"Friends are useful to have," Cadieux said. "I'll send a car for you."

"No," I said. "You won't."

"Pardon?"

"You heard me. I'm not letting you get your hands on me again."

"Poor choice of words, considering."

"I have what you want. I know how much you want what I have. We're going to meet somewhere you can't put a bag over my head, and where I can see you and Mason and Cody coming from a long way off. Somewhere public."

I could sense Cadieux deciding whether to start carving up one or both of his captives, just to regain the upper hand in the negotiations. Instead, he said, "When and where?"

"Eight tonight," I said. "The Cloud Gate."

There was a pause. Then he said, "Where the hell is the Cloud Gate?"

EIGHTEEN

"You're early," I said to Michel Cadieux as I walked up to the Cloud Gate, aka the Bean. At eight p.m. it was still reliably filled with tourists, which was exactly as I wanted it to be. He was there with Mason and Cody Williamson standing close by. I didn't see Cadieux's goons, but I assumed they were around somewhere.

"You're not," he said. I could tell he was piqued about having been forced out into the open. This, of course, suited me just fine. "Let's get this over with. Show me the crypto wallets."

I reached into my pockets and fished out both plastic squares and showed them to him.

He nodded. "Now give them to me."

"I'll give them to you one at a time," I said, pointing at Mason and Williamson. "One for one."

Cadieux stewed. "I suppose you want Mason first," he said.

I shook my head. "Cody Williamson first."

"What do you care about him, anyway?"

"I don't care about him," I said. "But he's still my responsibility. You get your wallet for him. Let him walk, and tell whatever goons you have out there that if he's not left alone, I walk with Mason's wallet."

"If I have goons out there, you won't be able to walk with Mason's wallet."

"Maybe," I allowed. "Tell them anyway."

Cadieux took out his phone, opened what I assumed was his HowlRound app, and sent a text. Then he put his phone back into his pocket. "Done," he said. Then he looked over to Williamson. "You're fired. Fuck off."

Williamson looked at me, unsure.

"You really *should* fuck off," I said helpfully.

Williamson walked, and then ran, down Michigan Avenue. We watched him go.

"Your turn," Cadieux said, bringing his attention back to me.

"Fair enough," I said as I tossed his crypto wallet to him.

He caught it, examined it, and then put it on the ground and crushed it with his heel.

"That's littering," I said.

"I can pay the ticket."

"What was on it?"

"Evidence of financial transactions that are best left mysterious. Now." Cadieux held out his hand. "The other one. This time you give it to me first."

"There's a complication here, isn't there?" I asked. "You need Mason in order to access his wallet. Just the wallet itself won't do. So I don't think you're going to give him to me once I give you his wallet."

Cadieux smiled. "I was hoping you wouldn't realize that."

"We have an impasse," I said.

"I think I can force the issue," Cadieux said. "Even here in public."

"I figured you'd say that. So I took an extra precaution."

"I told you not to talk to your cop friend," Cadieux said.

"It's not her," I said, and pointed behind him. "It's *her.*"

Cadieux turned to see Gabrielle Friedkin walking up to us, with her lawyer, Ricardo Gomez.

"What are *you* doing here?" Cadieux asked her.

Friedkin turned to me and motioned to Cadieux with her head. "I was going to ask you the same question about him."

"Here's the thing," I said. "I made deals with both of you for Mason and his crypto wallet. Ms. Friedkin, you offered more money, but Mr. Cadieux offered not to chop up my friend bit by bit. It was difficult to decide which deal to go with." I glanced over to Mason. "Sorry."

Mason shrugged and kept quiet. He knew his best option at this point was to shut up and see what happened next.

"So here's what I'm going to do," I said, returning my attention to the billionaires. "I'm going to auction both of them off, right now. Mason and his wallet. Whichever of you offers me the best deal wins."

"Gabrielle, we need to walk away," Gomez said.

"But wait, there's more," I continued, and pulled out my phone. "Because whichever of you offers the most for Mason and his digital wallet gets this, absolutely free of charge." I pulled up a photo and showed it to Friedkin and Cadieux. They both leaned in to look, and then drew away, slightly disgusted.

"What is it?" asked Gomez, who didn't see it.

"It's Paul Cooper's right hand," I said, turning it so Gomez could see it. He, too, shrank back slightly. "You know, the one needed to access his laptop. Which the police have from the night Cooper shot himself, but which they can't get into." I looked at Friedkin and Cadieux. "I'm guessing there's a lot of incriminating evidence on there about both of you that you'd be happy never to have get out." I pointed at the photo. "If you have this, it won't. Until then, *I* have it to make sure neither of you gets any ideas to do anything terrible to me or Mason."

"Where did you get it?" Cadieux asked.

"From the same little elf who helped me get your crypto wallet," I told him.

"You could've just pulled that photo off of Google Images," Gomez said.

"Very true," I said to the lawyer. "And even if I do have it, I'm not going to wave it around in public here in front of the Bean. That's why it's an add-on. But honestly, Mason and his crypto wallet are enough, because"—I pointed to Cadieux—"you're screwed if you don't get it"—I then pointed to Friedkin—"and you're screwed if he does."

Friedkin and Cadieux looked at each other uncertainly.

"I see both of you know only half of the story," I said. "I can elaborate if you like."

"Do," Cadieux said.

"Let's begin with the fact Paul Cooper was an FBI informant, and MoreCoinz is a big government honeypot for people doing ill-advised things with their cryptocurrency."

Cadieux looked unsettled at this news. Friedkin, I noticed, remembered to look shocked after a second or two.

"One of you knew this already, I see," I said. Cadieux shot Friedkin a look, but she had her face locked down again.

I took this as a cue to go on. "Let's continue with the fact that the venture capital fund Shikaakwa Partners, the venture capital fund you two partner in, is both a vehicle for laundering money and a slush fund." I pointed to Cadieux. "Your family has kept ties with some of Southeast Asia's worst people and happily washes their money for them. They gave you eight hundred million to clean, and you put it into Shikaakwa to do just that."

I pointed to Friedkin. "You took that money and used it to prop up the Fairwood Glen project, which your family had put you in charge of. The pandemic delayed construction, and it was already rife with expenses your family wasn't happy about. You couldn't let it collapse, so you took funds from Shikaakwa to cover the over-runs. Specifically, you've been dipping into Cadieux's eight hundred million dollars."

Gomez looked at Friedkin. "We *really* have to leave."

"No one's going anywhere," Cadieux growled. Gomez froze at this. Cadieux turned back to me. "Go on."

"I read up on Shikaakwa Partners," I said, looking over to Friedkin. "You made sure it got a bunch of good press when you started it. You said the fund maximizes its venture capital by investing in cryptocurrencies."

"Yes," Friedkin said. "So?"

"It's a good sound bite," I said. "But it just means the fund floods money into minor cryptocurrencies, and then sells when small crypto investors drive up the value of the currency. It's classic pump and dump."

"There's nothing illegal about that," Gomez said.

"No," I agreed. "That's where Paul Cooper came in. He gave Shikaakwa an inside track on which currencies were ripe for investment, and he could hype certain currencies in the MoreCoinz app. He controlled the market, and the FBI shielded him from getting in trouble for it."

"You knew he was an FBI stooge," Cadieux said to Friedkin.

Friedkin opened her mouth but I got there before she could speak. "Not at first. She always knew Cooper could help her pump and dump crypto. She only found out about him being an FBI informant later, right around the time Fairwood Glen started going underwater."

"How do you know this?" Cadieux asked me.

"Cooper told a friend. The friend recorded the call. Then he gave it to me."

"That's not a very good friend."

"Mr. Cadieux," I said. "You of all people should know how bad phone security is." I turned back to Friedkin. "When you found out Cooper was working for the FBI, you blackmailed him to hide the fact you were skimming from Shikaakwa."

"This is nonsense," Friedkin said to Cadieux. "The whole point of cryptocurrency is it's secure. The blockchain will always tell you how much is in it."

"Sure," I said, "if you understand how it works. But if you *don't*, then the guy who actually runs the market for crypto can get it past you." I turned to Cadieux. "Which is what Paul Cooper did, for a while. Gabrielle told him if he didn't let her skim, she'd tell you about the FBI. Cooper knew about the money you put into Shikaakwa. He knew it didn't come from the software you make." I looked over at Mason, who had been silent this whole time. "And Cooper knew what would happen to him if you, or your family, or your family's associates, found out."

"This is absurd," Friedkin said.

"And it might've worked if Gabrielle hadn't gotten greedy," I pressed on. "When Gabrielle was skimming a little bit, Cooper could cover. Cooper would manipulate some cryptocurrency down, and then put some of the Shikaakwa principal into it and pump it back up. But Gabrielle *did* get greedy, and Cooper couldn't hide it well enough. Gabrielle tried bringing new partners into the fund—that's why Brennan Tunney was there at the party—but Cooper knew it wasn't enough. So he did the only thing he thought he *could* do."

"He killed himself," Mason said, speaking up for the first time.

"No," I said. "Killing himself was instrumental, but incidental. He killed the crypto market he created with the MoreCoinz app. The app has a fail-safe—if Cooper doesn't sign in after enough time, the back end locks. When the back end locks, eventually the app stops working. When that happens, billions in crypto vanish. Before that, people will sell what they have rather than lose it. The value of those cryptocurrencies craters." I nodded to Friedkin. "You lose everything in Shikaakwa. Investors and the Feds audit your books. You get found out. You go to prison. Or worse."

Friedkin said nothing.

"Unless the back end of the MoreCoinz app gets unlocked," Cadieux said.

I nodded. "Which is why *you* want Mason's digital wallet, and why you need him to access it. You'll confirm you've been defrauded. Then Gabrielle is screwed."

"She's screwed if the MoreCoinz back end *isn't* unlocked, too," Cadieux said.

"Maybe," I said. "Unless she times the market like Cooper did—get in when the currency is low and ride the value up. She *wants* the market to crash, just enough. Then when it rises, she can get herself out of her hole with you. That's why *she* wants Mason and his digital wallet."

I clapped my hands. "So. Now that's all out in the open, let's get to the bidding. Who wants to start?"

Cadieux, Friedkin, and Gomez all stared at me blankly.

"No?" I said. "How about this, then." I motioned to Mason. "I happen to have a dispatcher here. How about I let the two of you discuss this between yourselves, and Mason will decide which of you has made the best argument."

For the first time in all of this, Mason grinned. "Nice," he said.

"Gabrielle," Gomez hissed. "We go. *Now.*"

"Oh, and Michel," I said. Cadieux jerked his head toward me, probably for calling him Michel and not *Mr. Cadieux.* "I agreed not to go to Detective Langdon, and I kept that promise. But I *did* tell Agent Andy Liu of the FBI everything I just said. He thought it was very interesting. And *he*, I'm sorry to say, told Detective Langdon. Because they're sharing information."

From around the Bean, several apparent tourists sprouted weapons, trained on Cadieux, Friedman, and Gomez.

One of the apparent tourists turned out to be Agent Liu. Another was Langdon.

Cadieux, Friedman, and Gomez put their hands up.

And then Cadieux did something strange.

He smiled.

"Do it," he said, loudly and apparently to no one.

A red dot appeared on his forehead, and then his forehead wasn't there anymore. There were screams and everyone dropped to the ground.

When I looked up, I saw Chicago police in the distance, wrestling a man to the pavement. Cadieux's assassin— or travel agent, depending on your perspective.

Cadieux was gone, clothes left behind.

He had traveled by bullet.

"Don't *you* even think about that," said Langdon, who was now straddled over Gabrielle Friedkin.

EPILOGUE

"Cadieux is missing," Langdon said to me the next day, during my break from hospital work. I was once again advising families against dispatching their incapacitated loved ones, and once again being frustrated that they weren't listening. I was ready for the Family Compassion Act to be repealed. No one in the Illinois statehouse appeared to agree.

"I mean, yes," I said to Langdon. "That was his whole plan when he had his flunky make that head shot with a high-powered rifle."

Langdon shook her head. "No, you're not hearing me. He's not just *gone*. He's missing. He's not here in Chicago, obviously. But he's not in Lyon, either. Interpol came to his home there not long after he was shot. His house was empty. And there were signs of a struggle."

"That's interesting."

"'Interesting' is a word for it. Interpol suspects some of his family's business associates may have heard about what happened to their money and were displeased."

"If I were defrauded of eight hundred million dollars I would be displeased, too," I said.

"You don't know who might've tipped them off?" Langdon asked.

"I have literally no idea."

"Just like you have no idea how a box of incriminating documents, as well as a picture of a severed hand, and a crypto wallet that had previously been in the possession of the Chicago Police Department, just happened to show up on your doorstep the moment they were useful to you."

"Exactly like that," I confirmed.

"It's nice to be owed favors," Langdon said.

I smiled. "And Gabrielle Friedkin?"

"In jail for now but probably not for long," Langdon said. "I can't imagine she won't post bail. Her lawyer, on the other hand, is probably in for the duration. He doesn't have her billions. Also client-attorney privilege doesn't apply when you're helping your client bilk hundreds of millions from your venture fund partners."

"No, I don't imagine so," I said.

"I imagine Friedkin's trying to find a way to pin it all on him. Billionaires are good at blaming things on their underlings."

"Knowing Gomez, he might suggest it himself."

"You'll be happy to know Paul Cooper's parents have been able to put aside their differences long enough to allow MoreCoinz's back end to be unlocked, with your friend Mason's help," Langdon continued. "They also gave us permission to use his hand to open his laptop and download the files there. I'm sure you know the hands showed up."

"I hadn't heard."

"In a box, left at the Michaelson Funeral Home. Along with its stolen van. You know, the one your friend Mason was seen putting Cooper's body into."

"What's going to happen to Mason?"

"You mean for body snatching?" Langdon asked. I nodded. "The parents aren't planning to press charges. Mason struck a deal with the Cook County DA. He assists with the case against Gabrielle Friedkin, he gets probation. Of course, one of the terms of his probation is that he's not allowed to do any more 'gray area' dispatching gigs. It's the straight and narrow for Mason Schilling from now on. Do you think he can do that?"

"If the alternative is 'or jail,' maybe," I said.

"I'd tell you to keep an eye on him, but given your magic box of evidence, maybe it should be the other way around," Langdon said.

"There's irony in that."

"We're still going to have that long talk, you and I," Langdon promised.

I nodded. "We will, I promise."

"Okay."

"And in the meantime, thank you."

"For what?" Langdon asked.

"For trusting me even when I didn't deserve it," I said.

"You were helping a friend, Tony."

"Yes," I agreed. "But I'm sorry I hurt another friend doing it."

Langdon smiled.

"I understand you have to be a good boy from now on," I said to Mason. We were getting ice cream at Zooaballoo, ostensibly to celebrate Mason no longer being under threat of mutilation, but mostly because I was in the mood for ice cream and it was close by.

"That's one way of putting it," Mason said. "I think of it more as my income range suddenly getting substantially narrower." He held up his ice cream, which was in the shape of a shark. "Thanks for springing for this, by the way."

"You'll find work," I said. "The hospitals still need dispatchers."

"Yes, thank God for the infirm," Mason said sarcastically. "And the bad judgment of their families."

"There's something I still don't understand," I said around my ice cream.

"What's that?"

"Why Paul Cooper gave you the access to his app's back end. Why you?"

Mason looked at me like I was simple. "He didn't give it to *me*."

"He literally put the access functions on your crypto wallet," I said.

"Yes, like you put a package into a courier bag," Mason said. "I wasn't the actual recipient. I was the delivery guy. When I finally opened up the wallet, under the watchful eye of Agent Liu—which was no fun, by the way—there were specific delivery instructions and a hundred-thousand-dollar tip to ensure my compliance. That was a surprise."

"Nice surprise."

"Yes, well. The Feds won't let me keep it. All things considered, I wish Cooper had told me beforehand. Then all this wouldn't have happened."

"It still would've happened," I said. "It wasn't about you."

"Then at least I would've found a way to make myself disappear *before* I needed to roll out of a moving vehicle," Mason said.

I smiled. "Who were you meant to deliver to?"

"Come on, Tony," Mason said. "Who do you think?"

"So, Brennan Tunney."

"Look at you. You can be taught." Mason stabbed his ice cream with his spoon.

"Okay, then why *him*?"

"Because Tunney found out Friedkin was blackmailing Cooper," Mason said. "He offered to intervene for Cooper. Gave him counsel. Outlined his options."

"Like suicide?" I said. "That's not exactly helpful."

"I don't think *that*," Mason said. "But crushing the market to hurt Friedkin? Sure."

"But giving *anyone* the option to unlock the app's back end meant the plan could be short-circuited," I said. "I don't understand why he did it."

"That's because you're not obscenely rich."

"Neither are you."

"Maybe not, but I get them and you don't," Mason said. "People who are motivated to make that much money are always thinking about their legacy. They get wrapped up in that shit, Tony. Friedkin and Cadieux have families to live up to. Tunney is trying to change his family's legacy. Cooper was creating his. His legacy was his app, FBI honeypot or not. When it came down to it, he *couldn't* destroy it. So he gave it to someone who understood what legacy means."

I stared at Mason. "Do you actually believe that?"

Mason shrugged. "Works for me. Anyway. Our little adventure has taught me that being a billionaire is a shitty way to live."

"You. Of all people, *you*. Think being a billionaire is a shitty way to live," I said.

"Don't get me wrong, Tony. I *love* money," Mason said. "We've known each other long enough for you to know that. But money is *for* things, it's not *the* thing. When it becomes *the* thing, it fucks you up. No one needs a billion dollars for things. And no one who's a billionaire is happy. Was Friedkin happy? Was Cadieux? Was Cooper?"

"No," I agreed.

"I don't need a billion dollars," Mason said, and then got a grumpy look. "But I'll tell you what, I'm going to need more than I'll make being a normal dispatcher for the next five years on probation."

"You'll live," I said.

"Yeah, I know," Mason said. "That's the only thing I got out of this whole mess."

He took another bite of his shark.

There was a black town car waiting for me when I left Mason at Zooaballoo and walked back to my place. The driver got out, opened the door, and beckoned me in. I peered inside. Brennan Tunney was waiting there.

"You're not in trouble," he assured me.

"If I was in trouble, you wouldn't have come to see me yourself," I said.

Tunney smiled and motioned me in. "Come take a turn around the block with me."

I got in. The driver closed the door, got back into his seat, and started off.

"I wanted to thank you," Tunney said. "For everything you did."

"You're welcome," I said. "But I didn't do it for you."

"No, you did it for your friend," Tunney said. "That's admirable. Especially for a friend who might not've returned the favor."

"I think he would've. Mason always looked out for me."

"When it's convenient for him, yes," Tunney said. "But I'm not here to question your loyalties, Tony. I'm here to show you my appreciation."

"What does that mean for me?"

"Well, what would you like for it to mean? I can offer you money, if you like. Some material thing you desire. A favor to be redeemed later. You squandered that last one, if you don't mind me saying so. You could use another one."

I shook my head. "I don't want any more favors from you. But you can do one thing for me."

Tunney opened his hands. "Name it," he said.

"You can tell me the truth."

Tunney smiled and spoke to his driver. "Take two turns around the block, Sean, please." The driver nodded. Tunney turned back to me. "For as long as it takes to go around the block twice, Tony, I will tell you the truth."

"What happened to Michel Cadieux?"

"I don't know," Tunney said. "But I'm reasonably confident some of his family's less forgiving business partners knew what happened to their money, and they knew Michel could be expected home soon. So I think nothing good happened to him when he arrived."

"Okay. Why did you take Paul Cooper's hands?"

"Sooner or later, the police would've remembered that corpses have fingerprints, and I didn't want any of the information on that laptop to come out early."

"Why'd you make Mason take the corpse?"

"I needed a second person for the job and he needed my protection."

"Did you know Paul Cooper had left control of his app to you?" I asked.

"I might've suggested it to him. I may have also suggested using Mason as the courier. I was pleased when Mason came to me asking for help. It meant I wouldn't have to extract that app access from him. Of course, it turned out I didn't need, or use, that control after all. I have you to thank for that."

"Did you suggest suicide to Paul Cooper?"

"No," Tunney said. "It's a mortal sin. I have enough Catholicism in my soul to shy away from that. But at one point in our discussions, I could see he was thinking about it, as a strategy option. He knew what would happen to him if Cadieux found out about the money. So he thought about going out on his own terms. I didn't turn him away from considering that path."

"Why not?"

"I could see how it might be useful for me."

"How was it useful?"

"I had a goal in mind."

"Which was?"

"In the short run, I needed to knock the Friedkins out of the running for a development I want in DuPage County. They were close to getting it instead of me. What's happened makes things much more difficult for them. The city, state, and Feds will be all over them for the next couple of years. That's bad for their business, and good for mine. In the longer run, this improves my company's position and takes us entirely into the realm of legitimate business. And as I explained to you earlier, legitimate business is a better economic climate for my family's interests. So much easier than being a crook."

"So this was all for money."

"Not all for money, no," Tunney said. "There are certain existential benefits. But certainly the money was a part of it."

"Mason was just saying how no one needs a billion dollars for anything."

Tunney smiled. "Perhaps. I think it's more accurate to say that Mason Schilling cannot conceive of the uses to which a billion dollars can be put. If one is patient, and one is not greedy, and one has the will."

"Like a development in DuPage County," I said.

"If you like." The car had come to a stop and Sean, the driver, got out. "I believe this is your stop, Tony. Thank you again for your service to me."

"Thank you for helping me help a friend."

"Of course." The door opened. "And Tony."

I paused on the way out. "Yes?"

"I figured you wouldn't want anything from me. So while we took these turns, I left a little something for you in your apartment."

I blinked. "You what?"

"It's in your safe. Allow me to suggest that you now, finally, change the PIN."

I got out of the car. Brennan Tunney was driven away.

Nothing had been taken from my safe. What was added was a crypto wallet and a note. *What you are owed*, the note read.

I stared at the crypto wallet for a few minutes. Then I took it out of the safe and into the kitchen, and laid it on the counter. I reached into one of the lower cabinets and removed the cast-iron skillet I'd bought when I thought I might ever actually cook something.

With the cast-iron skillet, I smashed the crypto wallet into roughly a hundred pieces.

And then I went to change the PIN on my safe.